West of the Cimarron

There was a job for Lance Turner if he cared to take it: that of the marshal of Vengeance. He would have to clean up the town of lawless elements and make it a decent place for honest people.

Lance took on the job, but the citizens forgot to tell him that nobody in town would back him when it came to a showdown with Wayne Patten, the big cattle boss, who claimed that he owned the town, lock, stock and barrel.

There was no posse in Vengeance, no one to ride out with him against the hired killers sent by Patten to destroy the marshal and prevent the town from becoming a peaceful place. Who could tame the trail crews, the gamblers and the professional gunslingers?

Then came the showdown with the lawless bands on the one hand, and a lone man on the other, a man who wore the star of the marshal of Vengeance on his shirt. . . .

West of the Cimarron

John Manville

A Black Horse Western

ROBERT HALE · LONDON

ISBN 0 7090 7216 3

Robert Hale Limited
Clerkenwell House
Clerkenwell Green
London EC1R 0HT

Typeset by
Derek Doyle & Associates, Liverpool.
Printed and bound in Great Britain by
Antony Rowe Limited, Wiltshire

ONE

BELOW THE
CIMARRON

Slowly Lance Turner pushed his weary horse along a high ridge, veering away from the rough peaks which towered over him, crushing down out of the steel blue of the sky. The sun overhead was a brassy disc, filled with a pressing heat, and he wore his bandanna over his nostrils as the dust from the trail, white and alkaline, settled over his face, rubbed by sweat into the folds of his skin. There was no chance of reaching Vengeance before nightfall, and he knew he would have to make camp again somewhere among the foothills where the mighty rush of the newly born Cimarron River splashed in a surging roar of foam over the rocks before it came out into the flatness of the prairies, where it took a smoother and more leisurely course.

Easing himself up in the saddle, he glanced back at the burro plodding with a slow, rolling gait behind the stud. All he possessed in the world was there. The prospector's tools, pick, shovel and the burro itself – and the three bags of gold nuggets which represented two years' hard work in the hills where he had made his strike. Two years of cold and heat, of a near starvation diet, long days and nights

spent alone in that wilderness. Now it was all finished. He
had done with the hills for good, was on his way down into
Vengeance to deposit his fortune in the bank there. In all,
he guessed it amounted to close on twenty thousand
dollars.

He sat hunched forward in the saddle, the reins held
competently in the slim hands, his body leaning and swaying to compensate for the rolling gait of the stud. A tall,
slim-built man, narrow in the hips, the single Colt tied
down at his hip. His keen blue eyes peered ahead from
beneath the brim of the floppy hat that kept the blazing
sun from his eyes. Everything except muscle and sinew
and bone had long since been sweated and worked off his
frame. He lifted his head and watched the slender ribbon
of the trail where it wound down the side of the mountains. Far below he could make out the flash of sunlight on
the broad river, knew that he could reach it that evening,
and he would make camp there. He had seen no one
during the whole of his two years in the mountains, except
for a couple of prospectors like himself from whom he
had managed to buy some supplies.

He wondered for a moment how well they had fared.
Perhaps they had found a rich vein as he had, or maybe
their bodies were lying up there among the rocks at that
moment.

He grinned wryly as his mind drew the comparison.
Then he began to think of what lay ahead for him. The
township of Vengeance which he had left two years before
when he had headed into the hills. Once he had deposited
his gold in the bank there he would have a bath, a change
of clothes, a shave, and then he would really begin to live.
He had lived too long up there in the wilderness. This
would be his chance to start a new kind of life.

The grin spread to every part of his face, not remaining
on his mouth alone, but it held a touch of loneliness and
melancholy, with something brooding at the back of his
eyes. Those long years had changed him. No longer was
he the same man who had ridden out of Vengeance, head-

ing north to the hills. The flesh was sunk a little closer to the bone structure of his face, the lines around his eyes had deepened, but his eye was still as keen as ever and the slim hands could still handle a gun as well as any man in the west.

The dust churned about him as he made his way down the switchback courses, down through the heat haze of the long afternoon with the pressure of the sun on his body, bringing the sweat out on his face. Then, shortly before evening, he rode into timber country. Here was a green world, where the shadows hung deep and unmoving among the trees, with the sharp warm scent of the pines in his nostrils. The sun never managed to penetrate the overhead canopy of leaves, but the heat was still there, clinging close to the ground. The stud made no sound on the thick carpet of pine needles, and there was a silence so deep about him that it pressed on him more strongly than any sound.

This was only the second time he had ridden this trail, but he was as much at home here as anywhere in the state. He felt hot and hungry, but he did not stop, even though the stud's head bowed with weariness, and even the burro's feet were beginning to drag.

When he came out of the timber country, into the open, among the lower slopes of the hills, the sun had set and the sky was already beginning to darken above him. There was a brilliant flash of red at his back as the last of the day vanished. Now it was a cool, blue world with a breeze blowing off the slopes of the mountains. He felt it cold and refreshing on his face, taking the sting of the day's heat from his body. The hills were still beside him, black and tall and bulky, and the air was full with the smell of them.

He reached the river just as it got really dark, as the blueness of the sky faded to black and the stars came out. The main trail continued up over a hump-backed ridge and, beyond it, he could hear the sound of the mighty Cimarron River as it thundered down the hillside, winding away in a slow curve from where he reined, overlooking it. Here, sheltered by trees, he made camp on a shallow, rocky saucer of ground, back a piece from the trail. The timber was old, first-growth pine, massive at the butt, climbing in a smooth line for perhaps thirty feet before it spread out into a thick canopy of branches and leaves.

Somewhere close by, at the base of the foothills, there would be a ranch, he guessed, and it was just possible his fire might be spotted from below. But the wind now had a cold bite to it, and he had no wish to sleep cold through the long night. He ate a meal of jerked beef and biscuit, washed down with coffee boiled over the fire, then sat back and smoked a cigarette, feeling the contentment of the end of the day wash over him like a softness.

Old Smokey and the burro were among the brush ten feet away, close to the bank of the river, and even though he doubted if he would meet up with anybody on this trail, he was taking no chances, and the bags of gold nuggets were under his blankets. He knew very little of this part of the trail, yet inwardly he felt no concern. All of his life he had known only the endless pattern of desert and tall, sky-rearing hills, of heat and cold and the deep, utter silence that came with the night. Since boyhood his proper place, his only home, had been in the open, with the sky above him, his accustomed place on the rim of a flickering camp fire.

He lay back in his blankets, staring up at the occasional star that winked through breaks in the foliage over his head. The years just past had not been easy. He had had to fight to scrape the gold out of the hard rocks, swinging the pick until his arms and shoulders had ached with the dragging monotony of it, fighting blizzard and snow during the hard winters, heat and drought during the summers. For close on a year he had found nothing. But there had been a bitter and stubborn pride in him which had refused to allow him to give in, although there had been days when he had felt like leaving the tools where they lay, saddling up Old Smokey, and riding back down the mountain trail, back to Vengeance, to admit defeat. Memory came up abruptly against the bitter knowledge of those long, weary days. They had hardened him, changed him. Then, one day in the early winter, he had discovered the rich vein that led back through the rock.

It had proved to be even richer than he had ever dared hope, and now the leather bags were filled with the hard, golden nuggets he had cut from the rocks, enough there to keep him in luxury for the rest of his life. Turning on his side, away from a stone that was grinding in the middle of his back, he closed his eyes and slept, with only the wind sighing and rustling in the harsh mesquite bushes in his ears.

When he woke again it was grey dawn. The stars and moon had gone and there was a glow beginning to spread up from the eastern horizon. Getting up, he put fresh wood and branches on the fire, waited until the flames began to pick about them, then boiled himself more coffee, ate a lonely meal. The silence about him was built, rather than lessened, by the sound of the river close by, racing and bubbling between its rocky banks. He watered the sorrel and the burro, tied his roll across the burro's back, then swung up into the saddle, urging the stud forward. Way back along the trail, higher in the mountains, the river, freshly born there near the summit, had been small and shallow, easy to ford, but here it was the best part of twenty yards from bank to bank, and in the middle, where the current flowed most swiftly, it was difficult for the sorrel to keep its balance on the smooth stone of the river bed, and the water pushed hard against the animal's chest as it thrust its way forward towards the opposite bank.

There was no need to worry about the burro. Heavily laden as it way, such a creature was as sure-footed here as it was on the winding switchback trails high in the mountains. Old Smokey struggled for a moment on the slippery stone, came to a full pause to gain balance, then moved on again, working forward through the shallows ahead to dry land, clambering up the steep side of the bank.

Pausing there, Lance glanced about him, studying his situation. The canyon here made a swift turn to his right, the left-hand wall remaining sheer as far as he could see. Where the trail suddenly dipped towards the rolling flatness of the prairie down below, the rough rocks of the ridge came down in huge folds of grey. It was a rough slope but, he guessed, a passable one. Now that he had crossed the river, he estimated that he ought to be in Vengeance shortly after noon.

Swinging the sorrel's head around, he made better time moving down the rough slope and, by degrees, the roughness of the country through which he rode began to soften. There were wide open spaces now, with no timber, and few rocks, with bare patches of ground that supported only the mesquite and thorn bushes and the tough, stringy grass which managed to suck moisture and life out of the barren soil which, here, had no depth.

Crossing the final ledge, he made out the cluster of buildings in the far distance, shimmering now in the heat haze of mid-morning. Another ten miles, perhaps, before he reached town. For a moment the old bitterness came up again in his mind, the old hatred of the world and its insolence, the feeling of not wishing to mingle again with his fellow men. Up there in the hills, away from everything, he had found a strange kind of peace in spite of the hardship he had been forced to work under. Now that he was riding back, the old distrust, the savage desire to set himself against men, came again. If he found the world to be still cruel, as it had been when he had cut himself off from it, two years before, then he would bide by those same rules, would mete out cruelty to those who were cruel to him. For a moment his fists were clenched tightly on the reins, the knuckles standing out hard and white under the flesh. Then he forced the feeling away, forced himself to relax.

He rode over the rocky, smooth floor of the ledge, out to where the trail grew broader and better. Presently he came out on to the road that moved out over the rich grasslands. He lost no time now, spurring the sorrel. Ahead the town materialised from its hazy background, a cluster of wood-frame buildings, lined along either side of the main street. Vengeance lay at the western end of a long, broad valley, the single street shining with heat in the harsh glare of sunlight. Most of the houses, he noticed, were bulked together at the southern end of the town, clustering there as if for protection. Closer at hand were the stores, grouped about a two-storey saloon and a hotel of the same height.

Lance's keen eyes sought, and found, the bank. It stood, logically, next to the sheriff's office, which was also the site of the jail. Maybe some day they would get around to building a new jail, but until that time, the prisoners were housed at the rear of the sheriff's office.

Down the slope into the dusty street he rode, conscious that eyes were following him all the way along. Men were seated on the boardwalks, in the shade thrown by the buildings. From the upper storey of the saloon a group of hard-faced girls, their lips painted a rich scarlet, stared at him with an open, appraising curiosity as he rode slowly by, the burro trotting docilely behind him.

He hitched the stud to the rail outside the sheriff's office, swung down from the saddle, and went inside. One glance had been enough to tell him that the bank was shut. Nobody would be at work during the full heat of the day in a place like this. In spite of the heat that lay over everything like a pressing, oppressive blanket, the town seemed to possess a bleak and unfriendly look. He wondered if any of the folk here remembered him. In two years a lot could happen, men went out into the hills and they never came back. People soon forgot a face and he had made few friends while he had been there.

Sheriff Jake Sloan was a big-boned man, broad-shouldered, with a heavy black beard which half concealed the puffy, heavily jowled features. He swung round in his chair as Lance went inside, ran his gaze up and down the other, before saying with a forced heartiness:

'Lance Tuner! Never figured we'd see you again around these parts. How long has it been? Two, three years since you rode out into the hills looking for gold?' The lower eyelids narrowed his eyes, giving him a mean, reflective look. For a moment his gaze swung away to stare through the glass of the window, to where the sorrel and the burro stood patiently in the dusty street.

'Two years,' said Lance tightly.

'Yeah, it would be all of that, I guess.' The other paused, then heaved himself up out of the chair. 'Say, you didn't find any gold up there?' The sheriff's eyes held a shrewd, speculative stare.

Lance's eyes narrowed at the veiled unpleasantness in the other's tone. Then he forced a quick grin. 'I found gold all right. Enough to last me for the rest of my life. I don't aim to be going back into those hills again. From now on I'm taking things easy.'

'Glad to hear it. So you finally struck it rich. Not many men around these parts can say the same thing, though they still go up there, year after year, still trying.'

'I noticed that the bank was shut when I rode in.'

'Sure, sure. They'll open again about three. I'm sure glad you came straight to see me, Mr Turner. It was the right thing to do. There's sure no point for you to go wanderin' around town with all that gold on you, rootin' for trouble when there's no cause.'

'All I want to do is deposit it in the bank, then I'll take my time looking around the place, mebbe buy me a small spread hereabouts, and settle down. I ain't aiming to cause any trouble in town if that's worryin' you.'

' 'Course not,' Sloan, said. He sat down in his chair again, swivelling it a little as he spoke. He had an odd habit of not looking at you whenever he spoke, so that he was staring off in some other direction when the words came. 'But it would be only human if you felt you wanted to spend a little of that money on the town. I'd quite understand.'

'I ain't going to lose that gold to any of the cardsharps in this town, Sheriff.' There was a certain hardness in Lance's tone as he stared down at the other. 'I'll get my gold into the bank as soon as it opens up at three.' He rubbed the sweat from his forehead. 'Reckon I might get a drink on credit at the saloon while I'm waitin'. It's dry, thirsty work riding those hill trails.'

'Sure, sure. If they question your credit, tell 'em it's OK with me.'

For a moment Lance's eyes, blue and hard, like chips of ice, held the sheriff's steadily. There was something behind the other's heartiness that he didn't understand. Sloan was nervous underneath his outward expression of calm. Then he turned on his heel and walked out, walking his horse along the street to the saloon. Even though it was afternoon, music came through the open windows and over the top of the batwing doors, music and harsh laughter, and the shouts of men. Lance was hot and he was hungry, and the dust of the trail still lay sticky on his face and thick in his throat. He tethered the horse outside, the burro nearby, easing the cinch on the stud. Then he pushed his way through the swing doors into the saloon.

There were men at the tables, some playing a game of monte, others drinking at the long bar. It was easy to pick out the gamblers there, men who came only to win the gold of drunken men, using marked cards or tricks known only to themselves. There were also hard-faced, painted women, with harsh, brittle laughs. They had come a long way, too, come with the frock-coated gamblers and the fast-shooting hired killers, who were busy trying to carve a niche for themselves in this corner of the west.

He took his place at the bar, laid his elbows on it and put his weight on them, watching the gamblers playing poker at the nearby tables. Gradually he was aware that they were watching him with an equal interest, and he turned his gaze away. 'The bartender brought him his drink, stood waiting expectantly while Lance rolled himself a smoke.

'That'll be twenty-five cents, stranger.' The bartender gave him a curious, sidelong glance.

'I've jest come from the sheriff's office,' Lance remarked. 'He said to tell you that my credit's good in this saloon.'

The other's black brows lifted. He said: 'Mebbe you're strange here, mister, but if Sheriff Sloan said that he must've had some reason.'

'Could be.' Lance brought up one of the bags tied to his waist, laid it on the bar and opened the string, taking out one of the nuggets. 'Think this might be the reason?'

The barkeep took the nugget, weighed it with an exaggerated care in the huge palm of his hand, jiggled it up and down for a few moments, then handed it back.

'Reckon it might at that,' he said with a new tone in his voice. 'I guess your credit's good here any time, mister.'

He left the bottle and glass on the bar in front of Lance, moved to the other end and busied himself wiping the counter with a thick red cloth. Lance poured himself another drink, drank slowly this time. There was a growing warmth in the pit of his stomach, but there was also hunger gnawing there and he knew that if he drank too much rye on an empty stomach he would be easy prey for anyone with a mind to see for themselves what it was he carried in those leather bags with their ends tied so tightly with string.

Slowly he let his gaze wander over the men in the saloon, but his thoughts were a long way away. He hadn't known that it would be so bad those first long months out there in the rocky, barren wilderness of the hills – that hunting among the rocks for the first faint glimmer of gold in the grey. But it had been bad and that was the main reason he was quitting now, when he had made a pile. The gold in those three bags was not bad for twelve months' work. If a man stayed with it out there, and if his luck held, he could make himself a good stake, a start that would put him well along the road to being rich. That was a man who didn't think. If you thought about it at all, you realized that there were damned few men who made a rich strike out in the hills, that even if they did, there were plenty of two-legged vultures ready to relieve him of it in any one of a score of ways.

The bartender came back, leaned his arms on the bar. Lance eyed him with a head-on glance. 'Where could a man get a bite to eat in this town?'

'Best place is the hotel next door. They'll set you up with a good meal.' His gaze dropped towards the bags at Lance's waist. 'Better watch those, mister. This town ain't been properly tamed yet. Still some lawless elements here who'll relieve you of them soon enough.'

Lance nodded. He moved away from the bar, heading towards the door. Just as he reached it a bunch of riders swung into the main street at the far end of town, drove their mounts headlong down the dusty street, guns blazing at the signs over the doors along the street, raising a blinding cloud of dust. Several of them emptied their guns into the air in front of the saloon, the noise crashing and echoing between the rows of wooden buildings. Lance eyed them with a detached curiosity, a tolerant amusement. There was no resentment in his mind as he stepped back a couple of paces, letting the doors swing shut in front of him, just in case a stray bullet might ricochet off the boardwalk and find a target for which the lead had not been intended. Men from one of the big cattle spreads, coming into town to let off a bit of steam, he reflected.

Through narrowed eyes, slitting them against the sunglare and the swirling dust, he glanced along the street towards the bank. It was still closed and he guessed he had time to get a wash, shave and bath, and then a meal before depositing the gold.

Leaving the stud and burro tethered outside the saloon, he made his way over to the hotel, feeling a bit self-conscious about his appearance as he walked up to the

desk. The clerk eyed him curiously as he went forward, put
on a faintly disdainful smile.

'You got a room here?' he asked tightly, aware of the
other's stare.

'Well – I'm not sure that we can—' The other broke off
and stared over Lance's shoulder. Turning quickly, Lance
noticed that a big man had risen from his seat behind a
huge potted fern and came forward.

'Mr Turner is a personal friend of mine,' said Sheriff
Sloan. 'See that he gets everything he needs.'

'Sure, Sheriff.' There was a new note in the clerk's tone.
He pushed the register and pen towards Lance. 'Would
you sign here.'

'Thanks, Sheriff.' Lance gave a quick nod. He had no
illusions as to why the other had done that. Sloan did not
look the type of man who would have any real friends, or
would need them unless they could be of use to him. And
a man with a small fortune in gold nuggets could be of use
to anybody. After registering at the desk, he made his way
slowly up the stairs, to the room at the end of the short
passage at the top. Opening the door, he went inside,
turned the key in the lock, and went over to the window,
staring out into the street. The pressure of the heat head
still lay over the town, crushing it, like a thick and tangible
blanket that prevented movement. A couple of horses
chomped quietly at their bits on the near side of the street
and, here and there, he spotted a dark shape leaning back
in one of the high-sided chairs on the boardwalk, loung-
ing in the shade. There came another volley of shots from
further along the street, the sharp echoes dying away
slowly in the still air. In spite of the emptiness of the street
below him, there was a wildness, an untamed quality hanging over this town that you didn't notice immediately you
rode in, for it wasn't until later that it really hit you
forcibly, not until you had mingled a little with the people
here and become a part of it.

He unbuckled the heavy gunbelt, then pulled off his
dusty, travel-stained shirt, going over to the dresser on

which stood the large bowl and the pitcher of water. The heat in the room had warmed the water a little, but it still felt cool and refreshing as he poured it over his body, rinsing away the stinging alkali dust that had worked its way into the folds and crevices of his skin, itching and irritating.

Taking the clean shirt from his bag, he slipped it on, leaving it open at the neck. The air inside the room was hot and heavy, in spite of the open window. He guessed that they did not have many people stay at this place; after all, Vengeance was well off the main stage routes, one of the frontier towns, a wild place. He wondered how much he could trust Sheriff Sloan. There had been something real shifty about that man, something he had not liked from the moment he had first met the other. Two years ago, when he had last been in Vengeance, it had been Sheriff Pardee, a straight and honest man. Maybe he had been too straight and honest for the folk who would have liked to take over the town, and he had been replaced by Sloan, a man who looked as if he could easily be in cahoots with anybody who paid him well. How Pardee had been removed from office was something it might help to inquire about, if he could get anyone in Vengeance who would dare to talk about it, dare to tell him the truth.

Outside, the street was still empty. A deep and oppressive silence hung over everything, like the stillness that came before a storm when the thunderheads built themselves up over the hills, and the haze lay thick and heavy on the plain. Something was going to break here – and soon. He felt a little wave of apprehension ripple along his back. Then he forced the thought away. It was probably nothing more than imagination, brought about because he had been away so long from this place and the haunts of men.

A man rode by in a buckboard, his shoulders hunched a little against the heat that struck down on them through the cloth of his shirt. Another dismounted from his horse at the far end of the street. Then, a moment later, there

was a sudden movement directly below him, the faint
murmur of voices as men, unseen from the window, spoke
together on the boardwalk. A second later he saw the tall,
thickly built figure of Sheriff Sloan walk away from the
hotel, cross the street to the office. He opened the door
and vanished inside.

Judging from the slant of the shadows, Lance reckoned
it was nearly three o'clock, that the bank ought to be opening its doors pretty soon. He knew he would never feel at
ease until that gold was deposited there and he had the
receipt for it in his hand. Going back down the stairs, he
noticed that the clerk was nowhere to be seen and the lobby
of the small hotel was empty. Something seemed to have
sharpened his senses now, and he felt the apprehension
begin to grow in his mind as he left the key to his room on
the desk and stepped outside. The sun threw longer shadows across the street now, but the heat head was still there,
heavy and oppressive. Lance's gaze lingered for a moment
on the stud and burro on the opposite side of the street,
then he moved sideways, around the edge of the hotel, and
it was then that something – some hidden instinct perhaps
which a few men have, warned him there was something
wrong. He heard the faint, stealthy whisper of sound at his
back, like a foot being slid along the wooden boardwalk as
its owner moved slowly towards him. He half-turned, hand
slipping down for the gun at his belt. But it was too late. He
just caught the shadow thrown by the sun at his side, loom-
ing over him, his fingers had just closed around the butt of
the Colt, half-drawing it from the worn leather holster.

Then something hard and heavy crashed against the
side of his head, just behind his left ear, sending him pitching forward into the hot dust, his senses reeling, Only just
conscious, he felt strong, rough hands grabbing at the
leather bags in his left hand, trying to tug them loose.
Savagely, with all of his ebbing strength, he resisted, tried
to keep his fingers tightly closed, kicked out weakly with
his feet at his attackers crowded around him. Through
closing lids, he saw that there were three of them, but his

vision blurred and he did not recognize any of them as they kicked and punched at his ribs and body, shoulders and face. Whoever it was, standing just behind him, swung again with the vicious weapon in his hands and it cracked hard once more against Lance's skull. His consciousness began to fade as he desperately tried to cling on to it. Dimly he heard the man behind him say: 'Got all three, Carson?'

A savage, twisting heave, and the leather bags were torn from his feeble grasp. The blurred shadow in front of him stood up, then kicked him hard on the thigh. A stab of agony lanced through his legs as he fell back on the hard, dusty ground.

'That's the lot, Jake. Sure he ain't got any more over in his saddle-bags on the burro?'

'He'd be a doggoned fool if he left any hitched out there, wouldn't he?' snarled the third man, his voice just penetrating the mists of unconsciousness as Lance fell back. He vaguely felt someone running their hands through his pockets, then with the last of his vision he saw the dark shadows move off into the distance, knew that he had been pulled out of sight of anyone in the street, that no one would have witnessed this attack on him, that these men had left him there to die, believing that he would succumb to the wounds they had given him. He knew that they had left the gun in his holster, thinking that he would never have the chance to use it. But sharp in his mind, blurred as it had been by the agony of the blows he had received, there was the memory of the three voices he had heard above him; and he knew that he had recognized one of them and he would never forget the other two. His attackers had been faceless men who had jumped him in the narrow alley at the side of the hotel, men who had then melted away into the distance, thinking to lose themselves in the town, leaving him for dead.

Consciousness left him and he lay there in the dirt, unmoving, legs twisted a little under him, his breath rasping in his throat and nostrils.

When he came to again the sun was almost down and
the air was a little cooler on his face. The narrow alley was
in deep shadow and over his head the sky had faded to a
darker blue than he had last remembered it. With an
effort he thrust himself upright, resting his weight on his
arms, feeling the stab of pain that shot through his chest
and the lower half of his body, the splitting ache in his
head. Gingerly, sucking air down into his heavy, aching
lungs, he felt the side of his skull. There was blood
congealed on the skin and he winced involuntarily as his
fingers touched the wound there. He sat for several
minutes, getting the strength back into his bruised and
battered body, then managed to get to his feet, swaying as
the blood rushed, pounding, to his head, holding on to
the nearby wall for support. The street in front of him
tilted and spun for several moments before it finally
righted itself and he could see properly again.

His mouth was swollen and his tongue moved rustily
against his teeth, the pain in his arms and shoulders
aching like fire along his limbs. For a moment his
thoughts stopped as memory came flooding back, and
close on its heels the feeling of sharp and uncontrollable
anger. He had walked into that attack like a greenhorn. All
that trouble he had taken to protect that gold, only to
have it stolen from him just at the moment he meant to
walk across the street and deposit it in the bank.

It was then that the thought came to him that those
bushwhackers had certainly known a lot about the gold.
They had known he was carrying it, they had also known
he had booked into the hotel and would be stepping
across the street to the bank the minute it opened. Gently,
he tested his legs, putting his weight on them slowly, grit-
ting his teeth as pain jarred along them. But there were no
bones broken, they had merely been badly bruised by the
vicious kicking he had received and, after a little while, he
was able to draw himself up to his full height and move out
of the narrow alley into the street. The town seemed to
have come alive now that the heat of the day was past.

There were plenty of townsfolk on the street, a couple of men on horseback rode past, but nobody paused to give him a second glance. As far as they were concerned, he was obviously nothing more than a drunk. The anger came to him again as he clambered stiffly on to the board-walk and moved in the direction of the hotel. He did not feel so angry at the loss of the gold, although it had taken him more than two years of hard work and discomfort to amass, he was more bitter at himself for having fallen so easily for that sneak attack. Savagely he gritted his teeth, saw the clerk behind the desk give him a curious sidelong glance as he handed him the key to his room and watched him walk painfully slowly up the stairs.

Inside the small room, he locked the door, walked over to the water basin against the wall and poured some of its contents over his head. It stung the scalp wound, shocked some life back into him, so that he lost the last fuzzy traces of unconsciousness. Some of the skin had been scraped off the side of his leg where the boots of one of the men had glanced across his thigh, and he bathed it carefully, sucking in his cheeks as the cold water washed the blood and dirt away. But at last he had dried it and there was only the wound on the side of his head to attend to. He sat in front of the stained, brown mirror and dabbed at it with a wet cloth, keeping his face expressionless as he worked. There was a savage and bitter sense of urgency deep inside him, the need for revenge on the men who had attacked him, but he knew better than to go rushing about town trying to hunt them down, to shoot it out with them. They might still believe him to be dead and would be a mite careless; or, on the other hand, they might take no chances, would be ready for him just in case he had survived that beating.

When he had finally finished, his head still throbbing a little, he got up and went over to the window, just in time to see the clerk hurry out, throw a quick backward glance towards the window of his room, then scurry across the street in the direction of the sheriff's office. He paused outside, then rapped urgently on the door. Lance watched him from behind the thin curtains, taking care not to be seen by the other. Evidently the sheriff was not in the office for, after rapping once more, the other hurried off along the boardwalk towards the saloon, where he thrust open the doors and vanished inside.

Lance knit his brows in sudden concentration. He had no doubt in his mind that Sheriff Sloan had been one of the three men who had attacked him. He had not recognized the voices of either of the other two, although he knew with certainty that he would recognize them if he heard them again. And it was just possible that the clerk had gone across to warn the sheriff that Lance Turner was not dead, that he was very much alive and might come seeking trouble.

He sucked in his lips, reached for the pitcher of water and drank all he could hold. At first, when he had recovered consciousness in that alley, he had felt an angry haste, but that kind of anger could never sustain itself for long, and it soon hardened into a fixed and terrible patience. The immediate desire to find and destroy those three men was still there, but he knew that he would have to find them and shoot it out with them, make sure that they knew who had killed them and why he had done it.

Then, when he had taken his gold back, he would ride out of this town and keep on riding. He no longer wanted any part of it. There had been too much violence and anger in his life, too many men facing his gun, shooting it out with him. Up there in the mountains he had found a strange kind of peace which he had never thought to experience again. He had imagined that, coming back to Vengeance would be different from what it had been two years before. But now he could see that nothing had changed, the old ways of violence were still there, men still died by a bullet or were struck down without warning in some alley.

Outside, the clerk came out of the saloon, stood for a moment on the street, looking up and down, then he walked quickly and nervously back to the hotel. As he passed below Lance was able to see the expression on the other's face, and a grimness entered his mind. The other was afraid, scared to death.

There was still a dull ache in his body whenever he moved, and he guessed that he had a couple of bruised ribs. Carefully he hitched up the gunbelt, checked the long-barrelled Colt, thrust it back into the worn holster, then stepped for the door, unlocking it and going out into the passage. At the far end there was a sudden movement. Swiftly he turned, hand streaking towards the gun at his side. Then he relaxed as he saw that it was the clerk. The other had moved up the stairs and was heading in his direction, had stopped in his tracks at Lance's movement.

Purposefully Lance walked towards the other until he had come right up to him. His gaze clashed with the clerk's and, after a brief moment, the other looked away.

'Seems you were in a mighty hurry to find the sheriff a while ago,' Lance said softly. 'Reckon there may be trouble?'

'I – I don't know what you're talking about.'

'Don't you? You wouldn't have gone running over there to warn Sloan that I wasn't dead, that I'd just come back into the hotel?'

TWO

COLT JUSTICE

Quite suddenly Lance's stomach felt flat and empty. Reaching out, ignoring the pain in his body, determined not to let the other see how hurt he had been, he grasped the clerk by the shirt, bunching it between his fingers, hauling the man close.

'Don't push me, mister,' he said ominously. 'I came riding into this town peaceable like. I didn't aim to make any trouble. But it seems that somebody wants to make trouble for me. If that's the way this town wants it, then that's the way it's going to get it.'

The man stared at him truculently but did not reply. Lance could see the abject fear at the back of his eyes, saw his gaze flicker down to the gun in the worn holster. 'I can beat it outa you if I have to.'

'Look, I don't know anything.' A pleading note entered the man's tone.

'No? Then why all the hurry to see the sheriff? Seems you didn't wait long after I got to the hotel.'

'I guessed you'd been hurt – bad. I thought there'd been trouble, and I wanted to steer clear of it. I figured if I told the sheriff, he might know what to do.'

'Sure you weren't in on this little deal yourself? Sloan might have warned you to give him the word if I should turn up.'

'Sloan told me nothing. Look, mister, I don't know you. The sheriff said you was a friend of his, that your credit was good in this town. That's why I let you have that room without any questions asked.'

Lance said softly: 'I reckon you're lying. But you ain't one of those three who jumped me, and I don't reckon you got the courage to be in on this kind of deal.' He released his tight-fisted hold on the man's shirt, stepped back a couple of paces. 'But I figure it might be better for you if you were to stay inside the hotel for the rest of the evening.'

'Sure, sure. Wasn't thinking of going anywhere anyway.'

Absently Lance eased the Colt in its holster, then walked past the clerk, down the stairs, out through the empty lobby. The cool night air flowed against his face, blowing down off the hills in the distance, taking the day's heat out of the darkness. For a moment he looked about him, standing absolutely still, keening the night for any sign of treachery. In Vengeance it was well to trust nobody. Always there might be a man standing in the shadows, ready to gun you down. A violent town which had not yet been tamed; one which might need a troop of cavalry to tame it.

Treading softly and carefully, eyes alert, gaze flicking from side to side, he went forward along the nearer board-walk. From the saloon came the sound of harsh, high-pitched laughter, of tinkling music from the piano. If Sloan and the other two were in there, they would have plenty of their cronies about them, ready to back them up when they made their play. That would be trying to fight them on ground of their own choosing.

He seated himself in one of the chairs directly opposite the saloon, leaned back, biding his time, eyes fixed on the swing doors on the other side of the street, the warm yellow light pouring out into the cool darkness. The minutes ticked away. The town still moved about him, still filled with that vague undercurrent of tension which could be felt, tinkling along every nerve of his body.

A small group of men came out of the saloon, moved off into the shadows, saddled up and rode out of town, taking the trail to the north. None of them were the three men he was seeking. He sat there with a tightening patience, feeling the dull anger begin to grow within him again. Once he got to his feet, feeling the urge strong within him to walk across the street, push his way through those doors, and shoot down the three men he felt sure were inside. With an effort he fought the impulse down and returned to his seat.

Then, suddenly, silhouetted against the yellow glow of the light, he saw the tall, broad figure of Sheriff Sloan. As the other stepped through into the street, two other men ranged themselves alongside him, thin-faced men with deep-set eyes, their faces shadowed by the wide-brimmed hats they wore. Each carried a gun in his belt and, in the shaft of light, Lance could make out the glint of brilliance on the star which the sheriff wore on his shirt. Perhaps it was the sight of that which brought all of the anger and fury back with a rush that threatened to overwhelm him, the thought that a man as crooked as Sloan should have been elected to follow in Sheriff Pardee's footsteps, that it was more than likely that the other had been killed so that this man might take over that job.

For a moment the three men stood together in a loose bunch, talking in low voices. It was a measure of their concentration that none of them glanced up and saw Lance move out of the shadows until he was less than ten feet away, standing spread-legged on the dusty street.

'All right, Sheriff,' he said softly, his words carrying in the stillness which had fallen over the town, 'and those men with you. Reckon we got a settling to make, here and now.'

He saw Sloan jerk up his head, peering forward into the dimness, arms hanging loosely by his sides, instantly alert for trouble. In that same moment, as if divining what the other intended to do, the two men with him moved slowly away on either side, spreading out, ready to take Lance from three directions if he went for his gun.

'Who's that?' called Sloan harshly. He seemed to have deliberately raised his voice to warn several of the bystanders in the vicinity. 'Step up here where I can see you.'

'You've got something that belongs to me, Sheriff,' Lance called sharply. 'Around twenty thousand dollars worth of gold nuggets. Reckon those friends of yours didn't hit me hard enough when you bushwhacked me in the alley and stole my gold.'

'Now jest a minute, mister.' Sloan was obviously playing for time. He had clearly recognized Lance the moment he had spoken. Now he wanted to have time in which to play things his way, take the man in front of him at a disadvantage. 'You know who you're talking to?'

'I know,' muttered Lance bitterly. 'A crooked sheriff who spends his time robbing men who come into Vengeance on lawful business. Reckon that Vengeance will be a cleaner town without the likes of you.'

Lance felt the tightness come to his belly, hardening the muscles, felt the empty coldness in his chest. Symptoms he had experienced before, which were no stranger to him. But his face was fixed and cold as if carved from stone, and his hands were perfectly steady as he waited for the other men to make their play. He knew that it would not be possible for him to keep his gaze on all three of them at once. That was what they were relying on. One of them would make his move soon and without warning, hand flashing for his gun, hoping to bring it to bear and to pull the trigger before Lance had a chance to turn and face him. There was no way of telling which man it would be. Deliberately he unfocused his gaze and the two outside men swam back into view again, even though he was staring straight at Sheriff Sloan.

There was a harsh, provoking laugh from the man on the left, but Lance did not turn in that direction. He knew then that it would not be this man who would try to shoot first. It would be one of the other two. In the stream of light that came over the doors of the saloon, he saw the sudden hardening of Sloan's features. A moment later the batwing doors of the saloon were thrust open and a drunk staggered out into the street. As if this had been a prearranged signal, as if they had anticipated he would swing his gaze away from them if only for the barest instant, Sloan and the man on his left went for their guns. Even before they had cleared leather, the Colt was in Lance's hand, the long barrel spitting smoke and flame, bucking against his wrist as he thumbed back the hammer twice. Sloan jerked forward as the bullet struck him in the chest, seemed to lift himself up on his toes as if trying to appear taller than he actually was, then he pitched forward on to his face in the dust, lying still.

The second bullet had caught the other man in the shoulder, spinning him round under the force of the leaden impact. He loosed off one shot that ploughed into the earth in front of him. Before he had a second chance Lance had fired again and this time there was no mistake, the man fell back against the wooden railing alongside the boardwalk and hung there for several seconds before sliding to his knees, then toppling forward on to his face. Even before he had hit the ground, Lance had flung himself on to his face, rolling and twisting sideways as the last man, short and slenderly built, tried to bring his weapon to bear. He fired two shots in rapid succession, and the second raked a red-hot bar along Lance's forearm as he fired from the ground. He squeezed off a fifth shot, knew instinctively where that bullet had gone, then brought his feet beneath him and thrust himself upright, standing there with the gun tilted to cover the man lying on the ground a few feet away. But the three men would never move again, and slowly Lance holstered his gun, thrusting it down into the leather holster.

Now there was movement on the boardwalk. Several of the citizens came down into the street. Lance stood quite still, the fingers of his hand touching the butt of the gun in readiness for any further trouble.

A man came forward, picking his way carefully over the

three corpses. He was a short, florid-faced man with mutton-chop whiskers and a thick moustache, a square-topped high hat on his head. He looked up at Lance curiously.

'I suppose you know what you've done, mister?' he said harshly.

'Reckon so,' grunted Lance laconically. 'I never did like crooked, double-dealing lawmen, and when one tries to take your hard-earned gold, reckon it's time to step in and do something about it.'

'You got any proof of what you've just said?' demanded the other.

'I guess if you go through their pockets you'll come up with three leather bags of gold nuggets. They slugged me in the alley next to the hotel this afternoon and left me there for dead. Guess I've got a thicker skull than they imagined.'

The florid-faced man said something to the two men standing behind him and they walked forward, bent, and went through the pockets of the dead men. When they finally straightened, they had the three leather bags in their hands.

'I suppose you could be telling the truth, stranger,' said the officious-looking man. 'These yours?'

'That's right. Brought them in this morning, meaning to deposit them in the bank. That was when I was jumped by those three polecats.' He held out his hand. 'Now if you'll just hand them over, I'll be on my way. Reckon it best if I was to ride out and keep on riding.'

The other shook his head. 'You wouldn't get far,' he said solemnly, 'not after shooting down Sloan and these two men. Wayne Patten would have his men on your trail before dawn. They'd hunt you down and kill you before you'd ridden fifty miles.'

'Patten?'

'You must be a stranger in these parts. He owns the Lazy K spread to the east of Vengeance. You might say he owns the town. Sloan was working for him, same as those other two. He won't like it one bit when he hears of this night's work.'

'Do you know how Sheriff Pardee died?'

If the other was surprised by the sudden switch of Lance's question, he gave no outward sign, merely nodded his head slowly.

'He was shot down in the street in cold blood by some gunslinger, who rode into town one morning, who tried to shoot up the bank. Luke Pardee went out of his office and was shot down before he had a chance to draw, his guns were still in their holsters.'

'And this man Patten was at the back of his murder?' grunted Lance quietly.

'I guess so. He soon had Sloan elected in Pardee's place. Nobody could prove any tie-in, of course.'

'Of course.'

It was a familiar pattern. If a man wanted to take over control of a town it was essential that he should have the law in his hands. A crooked sheriff, willing to throw in his lot with anyone who paid him enough, was the first essential.

After that, it was quite easy for a man to move in and set up his gambling dens, saloons and hotels. Then, almost before the honest townsfolk knew what had happened, they woke one morning to find that there was no longer any law in their town, and that the lawless bands had taken over control.

The other threw him an appraising glance, nodded as if satisfied about something. He said: 'Don't suppose you'd like to pick up that star and take over Sloan's job here? You look like a man who knows how to handle a gun, and we need somebody here who's not afraid to stand up to Patten and his gunslingers.'

Lance shook his head. He jiggled the bags of gold nuggets in his hand for a moment. 'I've got what I wanted. Reckon there's nothing in this town for me. I've seen enough violence to last me a lifetime. I aim to ride out of here and keep on riding until I meet up with some place when I can find peace and quiet.'

'That's a pity. I'm Will Benson, lawyer in Vengeance.' He indicated the tall, thin-faced man standing next to him. 'This is Clive Henders. He's the man you've been waiting to see – he owns the bank here. To be quite frank with you, we need somebody here in Vengeance to protect ourselves and our families. It must be obvious to you that there's no one here can handle a gun well enough to give Patten any cause to stop his lawless work. It's high time we had some law here like we had when Sheriff Pardee was alive.'

Lance stared down at the leather bags in his hand, then shrugged.

'I ain't cut out to be no lawman,' he said sharply. 'Reckon you'd better try to find somebody else.' He forced a hard grin that thinned his lips across his teeth. 'Judging from what I've seen and what you've just said, I reckon that wearing a star in this town is tantamount to asking for a bullet in the back.'

'Then you won't consider the job?'

'Nope, afraid not.' Lance spoke without any hesitation.

'I know there ain't much pay with this job. This ain't a rich town, not with Patten bleeding everybody dry. But we could stretch a point and make it, say, four hundred a month.'

'Sorry, not interested.' Lance hefted the gold into his left hand, turned on his heel and walked along the dark, dusty street in the direction of the hotel, leaving the three bodies of the men who had tried to rob him stretched out in front of the saloon.

He knew that the men were watching him as he strode away, could see their point of view, but Vengeance and its troubles were no concern of his, now that he had what he wanted. It was up to them to find some new sheriff, someone who was straight and honest and could stand up to this man Patten and his hired killers. This was a pattern of violence which had its counterpart in a dozen other similar frontier towns. It was nothing unique out here in the west. This terror was a natural part of a country that was trying desperately to grow up, to become civilised. The Civil War had brought a lot of violence with it, and there were too many men who still believed that the South had not been defeated, and even more who could not get the lust for killing out of their system.

Inside his room he packed his duds, checked the Colt at his waist, loaded the empty cylinders from his belt, then thrust it back into its holster. There was an aching tiredness in his body from the beating he had taken that afternoon, but he knew that he did not want to stay in this town another hour, was determined to ride out.

Five minutes later he made his way out into the street again, walked slowly over to the livery stable. A man drifted out of the darkness where the shadows formed around the stalls.

'You riding out tonight?' he asked laconically. 'Thought you were figgering on staying around for a while.'

'Changed my mind,' grunted Lance harshly. 'Too many things about this town I don't like.'

'Sure. Heard about the sheriff. Guess he had it coming.'

Lance stood for a moment in the stall, his hand resting on the flank of the sorrel, then gave a quick nod. 'Reckon he had.' He rolled a cigarette, lit it, keeping back in the shadows and, over the flare of the match, he eyed the older man curiously. There was no expression on the other's face, but his eyes were bright and beady and there was a look of sly intelligence in them. He guessed that the old-timer knew plenty about what went on in the town, that he saw everything, missed nothing. That magpie curiosity in his eyes told its own story.

Swinging himself up into the saddle, hitching the burro behind, Lance rode slowly along the main street of Vengeance, feeling the stillness and the darkness press down on him from all sides. He had reached the edge of town before there was a movement in the shadows. Reining quickly, his right hand flashed down for the gun at his hip, then paused an inch above it as a voice said: 'Hold it, I ain't aiming to cause trouble.'

Will Benson came forward, stood beside the sorrel, looking up at Lance. His face bore a serious look. 'Thought you might ride out tonight, Turner. Can't say I blame you after what happened in town today. Just figured you might have had second thoughts about that proposition I put to you.'

'Nope.'

Lance shook his head decidedly and a vague anger touched him. What right had these people to try to hoist this job on to him? he thought fiercely. Why couldn't they leave him in peace? He wanted no part of this town. All he asked for was to be left in peace. 'Go find someone else,' he said harshly.

The other dropped his hand away from the bridle, then stepped back. 'Reckon there's nothing I can say now that'll make you change your mind. Pity, because I had you figured as the one man who might be able to rid us of this lawlessness. Still, if you're just riding through.' He paused uncertainly, then shrugged his shoulders.

He was still standing there as Lance gigged the sorrel and rode clear of the town, heading east along the winding trail. Running downgrade, now through flat country, now along the crests of low ridges with pine on either side of him, the moon swinging low and yellow on the horizon, the stars bright and clear over his head. It was still five hours to sun-up, and although the anger he felt within him was a sharp restlessness that drove him forward, making him forget the aches and bruises in his body and the throbbing in his temples, now that he had killed those three bushwhackers, his mind felt strangely void and empty.

Riding, he thought of the warning Benson had given him, of the man called Patten who ruled the town of Vengeance, who kept it under his thumb by means of the terror he could invoke, sending in his gunmen whenever anybody tried to stand against him, and he felt a little of the worry seep into the back of his mind. A mile out of town he made a wide detour to take him away from the main trail. His way lay upgrade then for half a mile or more, with the land growing gradually less rough before he dropped down towards the trail again, his progress slowed by the burro.

Lance paused a moment to debate his position. If he took the trail he ran the risk of running into those men from the Lazy K ranch. He didn't doubt that Patten would know by now of what had happened in the streets of Vengeance; that the man he had put there as sheriff to make certain he had no trouble with the law had been shot down by a stranger riding into town.

Suddenly he jerked upright in the saddle. There was the sharp bark of a rifle in the distance, the sound carrying well in the night stillness, echoing over the hills. A moment later he thought he heard the sound of a shot coming out of the timber, thinned and short, and afterwards he heard the rattling of horses in the brush. All of this was somewhere ahead of him, well out of sight, but he reined the sorrel and sat tall and straight in the saddle, eyes and ears searching the night for any further signs of trouble. He was not sure just how close that outfit would come, and he did not intend to take any chances. Trouble seemed to abound in this territory. The noise in the brush ceased for a long moment and the silence grew deep and long.

When it was clear that the outfit was not headed in his direction, he raked spurs along the sorrel's flanks, urged the animal forward along the trail. Ahead of him was a low rise and he approached it cautiously. Those sounds he had heard had originated from the other side of that hill.

Riding slowly along the upwinding trail, he stayed within shelter most of the way to the crest, and the cool night wind began to flow around him more strongly, blowing off the hills.

The sorrel was still tired and doubtful of the trail and stopped frequently, but within twenty minutes he was at the top, looking out over flat, rolling country; a stretching grassland that was now dominated by the flames that leapt up from the blazing ranch house less than two miles away.

He crowded the sorrel forward, loosening the burro. There came the sound of two shots, close together, then even the echoes were lost as the wind shrieked in his ears, his body low over the neck of the sorrel, rider and horse blending into one. Again and again his heels drilled against the flanks of his mount as he raced it towards the fire. Now, as he drew closer, he could see that the flames had already taken a firm hold on the buildings, that the blaze had reached out towards the barn and the corn in a nearby field had also been fired.

Out of the corner of his vision he saw the small hand of men ride off towards the hills to the north-east, saw that some of them still carried the burning torches in their hands. For a second he caught the break of gunfire, knew that it came from the direction of the burning ranch and not from the band of riders. Halfway over the flat grassland, with a quarter of a mile still to go before reaching the ranch, he heard the firing die away into a silence that was made hollow by the racket that had gone before. Again he brought down his spurs, sorry for his mount as he did so, but knowing that he had to get there as quickly as possible. The horse's shoes struck hard against a rocky underfooting as he crossed the wire boundary where it had been trampled down by the band of attackers, then he was in the hard-packed courtyard, sliding from the saddle, feet hitting the ground softly, catlike, as he released his hold on the reins and ran forward, one arm thrown up over his face as the heat from the flames struck at him with the force of a physical blow.

Seconds before he reached the burning house a shot rang out and he felt the scorching blast of the slug as it whined close to his head. For a moment he halted, then plunged forward again as he glimpsed the dark shadow still crouched in the ruins.

'Hold your fire!' he yelled harshly. 'I didn't come here to kill you.'

The other either did not hear him or did not believe him, for a second later he lifted the ancient rifle and loosed off a second shot in Lance's direction. It kicked up a spurt of dust as he flung himself forward on to his face, then wriggled into the ruins, the smoke catching at the back of his throat. A wooden beam, blazing along its entire length, crashed down from the burning roof and landed between the old man and himself. He had a creepy feeling in his bones for a moment and a small second of panic struck through him. Then he got his feet under him, tested the floor beneath him, then plunged through the smoke and crackling flame in the direction of the old man. Eyes watering, he finally managed to locate him, crouched in a small, clear space behind the shattered remains of a window. Weakly the other tried to twist around, to bring the rifle to bear again, his finger still curled about the trigger. But there seemed to be no strength left in him and, with a tremulous sigh, he released his grip on the weapon and slumped back against the wall as Lance reached down, staring at the other through eyes slitted against the smoke and the flickering glare of the fire.

Every muscle in Lance's body was so tight that it began to ache, and the muscles of his legs were already constricting into cramp, but his mind was clear and very sharp as he bent, caught hold of the other and dragged him upright, hauling him back out of the room, back across the smouldering beam that blocked their escape, out into the cool night air that flowed about them like a balm. Gently he laid the other out on the ground. Moments later there was a sudden rending sound from the direction of the ranch and the roof crashed in with a savage roar and a rush of flame. Sparks showered redly in the air for a moment, were then whisked away by the wind.

The old man moaned low in his throat, then tried to struggle up into a sitting position, then grunted feebly as Lance pushed him back.

'Just lie still for a minute, old-timer,' he said quietly,

sucking huge breaths of air into his starved lungs. 'Nothing you can do now, I reckon. They sure made a good job of this night's work, whoever they were.'

Glancing down, he saw the other moisten his lips. His voice was querulous and shaky as he said: 'You ain't one of them, are you, stranger?'

Lance shook his head. 'I heard shooting back there in the hills and came riding as fast as I could. What happened? Why did they attack you like that?'

'Guess Wayne Patten don't need no reason for anything.' Bitterness crept into the other's weak voice. 'He's been trying to git me to sell my place for a coupla months now. Reckon he just got plumb tuckered out waiting and decided to send some of his boys out.'

Patten again. Lance stared out into the dark night to where the hills rose high and round against the yellow moonlight. There was no sound of riders now, no sign of them out there. He guessed that they would have ridden back to the Lazy K ranch once their dirty work was finished.

'You alone in there when they came?'

'Sure. I tried to hold 'em off long as I could, but there were too many of the coyotes. They came at me from all sides, fired the corn and then the house. Then they burned the barn. Reckon I'm finished now.'

'I guess the first thing to do is get you back to town and to a doctor.' Lance noticed the ominous red stain on the other's shirt, and pulled it away from the thin chest, exposing the bullet hole in the shoulder. It was probably less dangerous than it looked, but the oldster was bleeding profusely and he needed the wound tended to as soon as possible.

Carefully he slipped one arm under the old man's thin, wasted shoulders, ready to lift him up into the saddle. It wasn't going to be easy for the other, that ride back into Vengeance, and every jogging lurch of the sorrel was going to send a blast of agony searing through the other's body, but it had to be done if he was to live. The old man groaned as Lance lifted and at that precise instant a gun flared less than fifty yards away, among the shadows on the far side of the burning barn. Nearby, the sorrel's ears pricked at the sudden sound and he danced away a little, skittering nervously. As though that first shot had been some kind of signal, now others lanced out of the darkness, from right and left of the ruined ranch house, some from straight ahead.

Cursing himself for not having considered the possibility that the gunmen had circled the ranch and then ridden back quietly to make sure they had finished their murdering work, he dropped flat on to his face, one arm around the old man, pulling him unresisting to one side behind the horse trough that stood in the courtyard. His other hand reached for the long-barrelled Colt, sliding it clear of leather, hammer back. He fired twice at the first flash he had seen, heard the bullet strike wood, splintering it harshly. Outnumbered, he knew that he stood no chance so long as they were able to see him in the red glow of the smouldering embers of the building, and he could not see them in the surrounding dimness.

'Lie still!' he hissed urgently to the man beside him, as the other tried to struggle on to his feet. 'Keep out of sight. I'll try to run 'em down. It's our only chance.'

Slithering snake-like to one side, he reached the sorrel, thankful that it was still standing there, although several of the bullets had pounded into the hard-packed dirt close to its feet.

Smoothly and swiftly, he swung himself up into the saddle, clutched at the reins tightly with his left hand, the Colt balanced easily in his right. Narrowing his eyes to see more clearly in the pale wash of moonlight, he kicked his feet against the sorrel's rump. The animal leapt forward as if it had been shot, feet striking the hard earth, rushing straight out of the light of the burning building into the darkness. Deliberately, Lance drove it straight for the point where he guessed at least three of the bushwhackers to be hidden. Two flashes came as the men fired at him, but their aim was wild, no doubt they had been scared and surprised to see the great horse come lunging at them from the darkness. They broke, tried to flee when he was less than ten feet from their hiding place. A bullet nicked the sorrel's chest and it reared violently, almost unseating him. Desperately he clung on with his knees and thighs, then pulled hard on the reins, whirling the horse, firing swiftly and accurately at the three shadows that broke from the small clump of low trees and tried to run into the open ground. Two died under his gun. The third, yelling harshly at the top of his voice, stumbled and fell in the path of the sorrel. Lance heard the man's thin scream as he went down and the next instant the flailing hoofs struck him square in the middle of the back and he lay still in the dust.

Again Lance whirled the horse, casting about for any sign of the other killers. Several slugs whined dangerously close to his head as he lay low over the sorrel's neck. He fired at a running shadow, saw it melt into the darkness close to the ruined barn. It was impossible, in the darkness, to tell whether he had hit the man or not. From the other side of the ranch house bullets were coming still. Thoroughly angry now, with caution thrown to the wind by the savage intensity of his fury, he thundered over the courtyard, firing as he rode. The anger came up from the pit of his stomach, constricted the muscles of his throat, cording it so that it was difficult to breathe properly. He fired again until the hammer clicked on an empty chamber. Then he wheeled the horse, stared about him. There were no more shots coming at him from the dimness and, vaguely, he could hear the crashing of men plunging through the brush as they attempted to get away. For a moment he debated whether to pursue them, run them down and try to kill them all. Anger told him that was the best thing to do; but now that the immediate danger was past, caution was taking over control of his mind, and he decided against it, sitting tall in the saddle for a long moment. There came the sound of horses being pressed hard, moving off into the distance, and this time he knew they would not come back. They had had enough for one night. Riding back with the impression that they had only an old man with a rifle to contend with, then finding themselves up against a man who could handle a Colt as well as any man.

The tight grimness was back in Lance's mind as he swung out of the saddle, went back to the horse trough where he had left the other. The old man was still lying there, his legs stretched out in front of him, pushing himself up on to his hands, peering into the darkness.

'Did you git any of them polecats?' he asked harshly. His voice sounded a little stronger than before.

'A few,' Lance muttered. 'Right now, I guess this ain't exactly the healthiest place to be. I'm going to take you back into town, have the doc take a look at that shoulder of yours. Reckon he ought to be able to fix it up as good as new.'

'Don't know why you're doing this for me, stranger,' muttered the other hoarsely, 'I reckon I'm finished now. Nothing left here.'

'We'll talk about that later, once I've got you to a doctor,' Lance said firmly. He lifted the other into the saddle, then swung up behind him. The burro was still where he had left it, half a mile back along the trail. Slowly he rode back into Vengeance.

The dawn was greying the sky to the east, cutting a wide swathe of light across the horizon, by the time he rode into the main street. The town lay in silence in front of him. Only a single light showed in any of the windows. In front of the saddle the old man had slumped forward a little, disastrously weakened by the loss of blood. Lance nodded a little to himself. This was probably the best thing that could have happened. That bullet wound was sure to be painful, and in his present condition, in a world that was neither quite consciousness nor unconsciousness, the other would feel very little pain.

Lance had no difficulty in locating the doctor's place. It

stood in a small side alley that led off the main road of the town. Reining the sorrel in front of the low-roofed building, he alighted, rapped loudly on the door, at the same time holding the wounded man up in the saddle as he lay slumped forward over the sorrel's neck.

For several moments there was no sound and he rapped again, more loudly and insistently this time. Seconds later he heard the movement at the back of the door, heard a testy voice call out:

'All right, all right, I'm coming.'

The door creaked open and he saw the tall, stooped figure standing there, peering out at him.

'You the doctor?' Lance asked quickly.

'I'm Doctor Manly,' said the other after a brief pause. Then the other switched his gaze to the man lying across the saddle, and he stepped out into the open, pulling the thin cotton robe more tightly around him as the cold air struck at his body.

'Who's this? What happened?'

'He's been shot in the shoulder,' replied Lance brusquely. 'I reckon he needs urgent attenntion. The slug's still there.'

'All right. Bring him inside, but if he's one of the Lazy K gang then I want nothing to do with him.'

Lance took the old man's weight over his shoulder and carried him into the house, surprised at how light the old fellow was. There seemed to be scarcely any flesh on his bones. Inside the front room the doctor lit a paraffin lamp and placed it on the table, motioning to Lance to put the injured man in the chair by the glowing embers of the fire. Then Manly stepped forward, tilted back the old man's head and said in surprise:

'Why, it's Herb Keene. How did this happen?' Even as he spoke, he went over to the side of the room, began taking out his instruments and the tall bottle of antiseptic.

'I was riding out along the trail when I heard shooting,' Lance explained. 'I got there just in time to discover that the ranch house had been fired, along with the barn and a field of corn. This old fellow was inside the house. He took a couple of shots at me as I went in to get him out, probably thought I was one of the bunch that attacked him. They came back while I was trying to help him and we had to fight 'em off. Then I brought him back here.'

The other turned and laid out his instruments on the top of the wooden table. Then he glanced up at Lance and there was a vague look of recognition in his eyes. 'Aren't you the man who shot down the sheriff and those two henchmen of his?'

'That's right. I'm Lance Turner.'

The other grunted. 'You're a fool coming back like this. I suppose you know that, especially if you've killed any more of Patten's men and helped Keene here. Patten isn't going to take kindly to anybody interfering with his plans like this. He'll send his men into town gunning for you before midday.'

'Seems that this hombre Patten has got this town on a string,' Lance declared. He stood beside the table and watched as the other ripped away the blood-stained shirt from the old man's shoulder and bathed the wound with the antiseptic.

'You won't find anybody here who dares to go against him. I reckon Herb was one who tried, and you see now where it got him. There's no law and order in Vengeance any longer, Mr Turner. And so long as Patten is allowed to go on like this with nobody lifting a hand to stop him, there isn't likely to be any.'

Manly gently eased Keene's body back, then picked up the metal probe. In the light from the lamp, Lance saw that the old-timer was unconscious now. Carefully the doctor began to probe for the bullet, his face hard and determined.

'Why should anybody want to kill a man like that?' Lance asked, as the silence in the room grew long.

'Patten has been trying to buy up most of the small outfits in this territory. Herb was one who refused to sell

and refused to give in to threats. I tried to warn him only
a week ago that there'd be trouble if he tried to go against
Patten, but he's a proud and stubborn sort of cuss and he
wouldn't listen. Now you see where his pride got him.'

'Don't you reckon that if everybody here banded
together, they ought to be able to stop Patten and his army
of killers?'

'Try to tell the townsfolk that and see where it gets you,'
said the other, with a trace of bitterness in his tone. He
probed more deeply, then exhaled in a loud sigh, dropped
something hard and metallic into the tray beside him.
'That's out anyway,' he said quietly. 'Now all I have to do is
bandage it up and keep him quiet for a couple of weeks.
By rights, he ought to have been dead by now. He's an old
man, and losing all of that blood didn't help matters any.'

Lance nodded, tightened his lips into a thin harsh line.
Through the window he saw the dawn beginning to
brighten in the street, touching the low buildings with a
grey light. Death and danger were becoming personal
things in this town now, he reflected quietly. The sleeping
anger awoke in him again as he straightened up and
walked slowly towards the door. His faith in human nature
had waned a lot since he had ridden down out of the tall
hills into Vengeance, expecting only to have to deposit his
gold in the bank there and try to pick up the threads of his
life where he had left off two years before. Now he knew
that this was quite impossible.

Reaching the door, he opened it and stood in the opening for several moments, drawing the sharp-smelling air of
early morning down into his lungs. He was aware that the
doctor was watching him closely from behind. In front of
him the town still seemed to be asleep, but he guessed that
this was only an illusion, that underneath the silence there
was a wakeful unease, a feeling that something was going
to break very soon. The breathless hush before the piling
thunderheads broke into a storm.

There was a peculiar sense of excitement in him now,
something he had not felt for a long time. Behind him,

Doc Manly said harshly: 'I reckon Keene needs a place to stay, Turner. You got any place in mind?'

'He ain't my responsibility now,' grunted Lance. 'Can he stay here for a while, until that shoulder of his heals up?'

A pause, then Manly went on, as Lance turned to face him: 'Sure, I guess so. I don't reckon he has any place of his own now.'

'That's what I figured. Could be that Patten may decide to ride into town and come looking for him. What would you do then?'

'You think that's likely?'

Lance pursed his lips. 'Could be. Those men of his would know that he's probably still alive, and they'll report to Patten once they get back to the Lazy K. Mebbe he'll figure that the old fellow can't harm him any more, but on the other hand, if he reckons Keene can stir up any trouble for him here in Vengeance, it's a sure thing he'll send some of his boys riding for him.'

'Then maybe it wouldn't be such a wise thing after all.'

'So you're scared of Patten, too,' Lance said briefly.

A humourless grin spread over the other's thin features. The drooping grey moustache curled a little, but there was no expression of defiance on the doctor's face. 'I ain't denying that, young fella,' he agreed. 'I've seen a lot happen here in Vengeance and I know enough to realize that unless we get a man who can use his guns fast and who doesn't bother to ask questions too often before he shoots, everybody is going to be scared of Patten.'

'Don't any of you realize what Patten is trying to do?' growled Lance harshly. 'Or are you so blind that you don't see the plan he's made? He knows that if everybody sticks together, if you all act at once, he's finished. Even with those gunmen he's hired to protect him and carry out his orders, he won't stand a chance if you all have it out with him, force the showdown yourselves. But right now you're playing into his hands. He's taking you one by one, and that way you don't stand a chance of defeating him.'

'It ain't easy to tell the people in Vengeance that,' said the other, a trifle sourly. 'They all saw Sheriff Pardee shot down before he had a chance to draw, and anybody else who's tried to stand against Patten has had the same kind of treatment. We aren't gunmen here in Vengeance, Mr Turner. We're all just ordinary, peace-loving citizens who want nothing more than to be left alone to live our lives in our own way without hindrance from anyone else.'

'And you figure that you'll ever get that by letting him walk in and take over everything he wants?' There was naked scorn in Lance's voice, a hardening sense of determination and decision in his mind, as he faced the other, then let his gaze switch to the man who lay in the chair, the blood-soaked shirt hanging from his bandaged shoulder. A man who had tried, alone and unaided, to stand up to the ruthless might of armed gunmen, professional killers who lived by the code of the gun.

Turning on his heel, he strode towards the door again, halted on the sidewalk as the doctor called after him, coming forward into the doorway:

'What are you figuring on doing now, mister? Riding back out of town? If you are, I suggest that you take the west trail, then circle through the hills about twenty miles to the north if you want to miss any of the Lazy K bunch.'

Lance shook his head slowly. There was a curious glint in his eyes as he said tightly: 'I've just decided to take the job of marshal here, Doc.'

THREE

MARSHAL OF VENGEANCE

He ate breakfast in the hotel, noticed with a faint sense of satisfaction the look of surprise written plainly on the clerk's face as he had strode in and asked for his room again. When he had eaten, he felt a little better. The aches and bruises in his body no longer troubled him quite so much, and even the wound on his scalp had ceased to throb so intensely. Striding across the street, he went straight to the small, glass-fronted office whose faded lettering told him that this belonged to William Benson, lawyer and notary.

Pushing open the door with the flat of his hand, he went inside. The room was much as he had expected. There was the smell of musty books and dust everywhere, and very little sunlight seemed to penetrate into the dim corners. The room was empty, but a moment later the door at the rear opened and Benson came in, wiping his mouth with a white napkin.

'Mr Turner,' he said, and there was a trace of surprise in his tone. 'I hardly expected to see you again in Vengeance.'

Grimly, Lance said: 'I ran into a little trouble last night along the trail.'

47

'Just so.' The other nodded, pushed the napkin out of sight and came forward. There was a speculative look in his eyes. 'Some of Patten's men?'

'I reckon so, but I'm not sure. They attacked an old man called Keene, fired his ranch and barn, did their best to finish him, too. Had to bring him back into town to the doctor. He's sleeping peacefully now, I reckon, but there was a bullet in his shoulder and he's lost a lot of blood.'

'Herb Keene.' The other nodded his head slowly, and there was no surprise in his tone. 'I've been expecting something like that for a while now. Patten wanted to buy that ranch and land. Even came to see me and asked me to have a talk with Herb, to try to get him to accept the money Patten offered.'

'And did you talk with him?'

'Naturally. That's my business here. But Herb, as I had expected, wanted nothing to do with it. He's a stubborn man.'

'And now he's been wounded and all of his possessions destroyed by Patten.' Lance sucked in his lips.

'Do you care what happens to anyone around here?' The other's tone was quiet and deliberately emotionless. 'Maybe not. And I'll tell you why. Because you've brought all of this trouble on yourselves. You can't blame Patten for it. He's just the greedy, avaricious man who'll get what he wants anywhere in the territory where the townsfolk are so scared, so like sheep, that they refuse to accept the facts and won't stand up against evil, no matter in which form it shows itself.'

'I asked you yesterday if you'd be prepared to take the job of marshal of this town,' said the other softly, almost as if he had not heard what Lance had just said. 'Now that you're back in Vengeance, I don't suppose you'd change your mind?'

'I've been thinking things over ever since I ran into Herb Keene. I'm not doing this for you, and I'm not taking the job because I like Vengeance, or what it stands for. And we'd better get something straight right now. I'll clean up this town for you, but on my terms. I'll do it my way or not at all. Is that clear?'

'Very well, I accept. I'm sure the others will, too. If Vengeance is to become a place where people can live in peace, then we've got to have some form of law and order and one that isn't run by a man like Patten.'

Lance gave a brisk nod. Inwardly he still wondered if he was doing the right thing. It seemed incredible that so much could have happened in the two days since he had taken that trail leading down out of the hills and ridden into Vengeance, seeking only to deposit his gold in the bank and then take his place in society there. He had never, for one moment, imagined that he would be taking the job of town marshal, seeking to keep law and order in the face of a menace such as Wayne Patten represented. He certainly didn't exactly want the marshal's job, of that he felt sure. He was sickened by killing and violence. All he had wanted to do the previous night had been to take the trail that led east, and to keep on riding until he came to a place where there were no such things as crooked sheriffs and greedy, avaricious men such as Wayne Patten.

'I reckon that as the lawyer here and in the absence of anybody else to do the job, I've got the authority to swear you in, Turner. If you'd care to step over to the sheriff's office, I'll do that right now. There's going to be trouble soon, I'm sure of it. Once Patten gets to hear of this—' He left the rest of his sentence unsaid, but Lance could guess at what he meant.

Together they made their way to the empty sheriff's office in the middle of the long, winding street. As they walked, their feet making hollow sounds on the wooden boardwalk, Lance was aware of the many curious glances that were thrown in their direction. He could guess what most of the townsfolk were thinking, knew it himself; that wearing a star in this town, unless you had been appointed to the job by Patten himself, meant you were a walking target for any trigger-happy gunman sent into town from the Lazy K ranch.

His face was sober as he followed Benson into the office. Sunlight shafted through the wide window, touched the dust motes in the air. Benson went around to the back of the long wooden desk, opened one of the lower drawers, then came up with a badge in his hand. He held it out towards Lance. 'This belonged to Sheriff Pardee,' he explained. 'I thought you might like to wear this one and not that which Sloan wore.'

Lance nodded, slipped the star on to his shirt.

Benson said: 'I'll get a contract drawn up for this afternoon. In the meantime, you can take it that you're hired as marshal. Thinking of swearing in any deputies?'

'You reckon anybody might take the job?' It was a direct question, but he saw the other's gaze slide away as if afraid to meet his eyes.

'Maybe not. Any man who took that job wouldn't last five days here. They all know it.'

'Then I guess I'm on my own.' Lance's voice was toneless. He nodded curtly. 'I half expected it. I don't reckon this job of mine is going to make me very popular around town. Because once Patten tries anything, the townsfolk will be busy running and looking after their own skins, they won't have time to back me up in anything I try to do.'

'Now, see here,' began the other harshly. 'You've got to be able to see our point of view. You can't ask men who scarcely know how to handle a gun to face up to professional killers like those that Patten has hired.'

'Nope, I guess not.' Lance felt suddenly tired. The nagging doubt had grown stronger in his mind over the past few minutes, but he knew that he could not back out of the deal now, even though he had not signed any contract yet making his appointment legal.

How would Patten react? he wondered. Would he come riding into town at the head of a band of killers and shoot up the place – or would his approach be more subtle than that? Lance wished that he knew. It would make all the difference to the way he acted.

'Well, I reckon that's all I can do for the moment.' Benson pushed back his chair, got to his feet and walked around the side of the desk. 'This is your office now, Marshal. Make yourself at home here. There are half a dozen cells at the back along that passage there, just in case we do get any unruly elements in town.'

'From what I know of Patten and his bunch, I reckon there's going to be only a few of them filled. They'll play for keeps when they do come.'

Benson nodded, then hurried from the office. Through the dusty window, Lance watched him hurry along the boardwalk, then vanish inside the saloon. There was no doubt that Benson was still a very worried man. He went over to the desk and seated himself behind it, looking about him carefully. There was still a little of the anger in his mind. These people had simply sat back and watched their town go wild and had not even bothered to do anything about it. They had seen Pardee shot down in cold blood, and had done nothing to avenge his death, even though they must surely have known that Patten had been the man who had engineered the killing.

Why hadn't they attacked then, cleaned up the territory before Patten could get a hold there? That had been the logical time to do something about it, rather than let the years slip by, let Sloan take over the job of sheriff, run the town his way on direct orders from Patten.

He sighed, leaned back in the chair and forced himself to relax. The sunlight slanted in through the window, throwing a pattern of light and shadow on the floor, heating up the air inside the office.

Acting on impulse, he got to his feet and walked along the narrow passage to the rear of the building. The cells there were ranged on either side of the corridor with thick steel bars set in the heavy stone of the floor. There was a narrow, barred window in each with a bench ranged lengthwise along one wall and a bunk with a solitary blanket in each cell. Evidently whoever had built and designed this place had been expecting trouble in the town, he thought with a wry amusement.

Going back into the office, he paused at a sudden shout from outside. Some sixth sense seemed to warn him that trouble had already started as he strode to the door, jerked it open and stepped outside, his right hand hovering very close to the butt of the Colt at his waist.

A tall, powerfully built man had ridden up to the office and now sat in the saddle in the middle of the street, staring at him, sitting his mount with a deceptive ease. Inwardly, at that moment, Lance could feel the tension that crackled in the still air along the whole length of the street. It was as if the entire town had stood still, was holding its breath, waiting with an expectant hush for something to happen.

'You Turner?' called the big man harshly. There was a calculated arrogance in his voice and bearing that was clearly designed to provoke.

'That's right.' Lance slitted his eyes against the sun, aware that he had been caught at a disadvantage there. He kept his voice deliberately steady, stepping forward a couple of paces down into the street.

'I hear they've elected you marshal in place of Sloan. Seems they could have picked a better man.'

Still Lance kept his temper, realizing that the other was trying to bait him, trying possibly to goad him into going first for his gun. 'Maybe you mean they should have asked Patten first? Seems they've been doing that far too long in this town. The marshal is elected by representatives of the people, not by a rancher who seems to want to take the law into his own hands. Could be that the people here have had enough of that.'

'You've made a big mistake, mister,' rumbled the other. He slid from the saddle, came forward, walking with a catlike tread in spite of his tremendous bulk. Lance knew instantly that here was a man who was a dangerous opponent, a man who would, in any fight, use every dirty trick in the book.

'Just what is your interest in this?' Lance asked.

'Let's say that Sloan was a friend of mine. That I don't
like it when anyone who's my friend is shot down in a
gunfight, and that I promised myself I'd take his killer
apart with my bare hands.'

It was simply said, but each word carried the promise of
death. Another step and the other came forward once
more, his eyes never leaving Lance's face. Deep down
inside, Lance knew that he could outdraw the other, knew
that this man was also aware of that, which was why he had
made no attempt to go for his gun. He wanted the advantage on his side, wanted to be able to use his weight and
strength and his knowledge of in-fighting, Ponderous,
monstrous, a brute of a man who came forward relent-
lessly. When he was still ten feet from where Lance stood,
he lowered both hands and undid his gunbelt, letting it
drop into the dust at his feet.

'Just in case you're figuring on shooting me down in
cold blood, Marshal,' he said jeeringly, 'I'm going to show
this town what kind of a man they have for a lawman.'

For a moment Lance hesitated, but only for a fraction
of a second. Then, lowering his hands, he undid the belt
and dropped it into the dirt, stepping back from it,
circling the man in front of him, dimly aware that a crowd
had gathered and that all eyes were on them. This was
either going to make or break him as the marshal, he
thought tightly. If he failed here, even if this man did not
kill him, he would no longer be able to enforce law and
order in Vengeance. Not only would Patten be able to
move in and take over whenever he wished, but the people
would never back him up when trouble came.

The man's hunger for a fight was clearly seen in his eyes
and the tight shape around the corners of his mouth. He
squared himself at Lance. He said throatily:

'If you're figgering on any of the folk in this town to
stand with you, Marshal, and help you, then you're—'

He never finished what he had meant to say. It had
just been a feint to cover what he aimed to do, for he
swung his right hand all the way from his belt, aiming

the solid blow for the tip of Lance's chin. If it had landed, it would almost certainly have finished the fight there and then, but Lance had seen the look in the man's eyes a moment before he had moved, had been ready for him. A split second before it could connect he swayed back easily and the man stumbled heavily forward, temporarily off balance. Even as he lunged in his direction, Lance hammered a couple of blows off the man's head, vicious, chopping blows, one of which smashed the man's nose, sending blood spurting over his grinning face. The other grunted, swayed back on to his feet and stopped dead, sucking air down into his chest, eyes narrowed in hate. Lance hit him with another piston-like stroke as hard as he could, felt his knuckles smash on the man's chin. It was like hitting a solid piece of granite. Pain jarred redly along his arms and up into his shoulders.

Savagely, the other came forward, seeming to ignore the blows that Lance had rained on him. He seemed indestructible, unmovable, smiling grimly as he came on. There was a deep, slow silence in the street now, as if the town waited with bated breath, wondering what was coming next. The big man's eyes glittered with the killing fever as he crowded after Lance, arms held wide now, seeking to grip them around his opponent's body, to draw him into an ever-tightening circle of flesh and muscle.

Very slowly and carefully, Lance edged backward, waited until the other rushed in, then swung hard again with his left fist. It caught the man on the side of the head, just behind the ear, but although he staggered a little, the blow did not fell him, did not seem to bother him too much. He narrowed his eyes a little, then feinted to his left, swung hard with his right arm. Taken by surprise, Lance could only hope to ride the savage blow. He took most of the force on his upraised elbow, but the other's rock-hard fist smashed against his chest, driving all of the air from his lungs. Swiftly, instinctively, he blinked his eyes several times in an effort to clear his blurring vision.

The man's face swam and wavered in front of him tantalisingly as he attempted to focus on it.

It came to him then that the other was not going to be satisfied until he had killed him. Another hard blow on his head sent him sprawling back on to the dusty street. He fell on his shoulder blades, guessed what was coming next and rolled swiftly, instinctively, to one side as the man came leaping in, kicking downward with his booted heels, hoping to thrust the rowels of his spurs into Lance's face, to grind it into the dirt.

The kick missed him and the man half fell as he slipped off balance. There was a throbbing roar in Lance's ears and he knew that he had to get to his feet, had to fight on, or it would be all over for him. Dimly he was aware of the heavy beating of his heart as it thudded against his ribs. It felt as if his chest had been caved in by that monstrous blow and every breath he took sent agony shooting through his body. He had the odd feeling that there were two men facing him, but knew that it was merely an illusion brought on by that blow which had temporarily affected his sight. With a supreme effort, he pushed himself to his feet, waited as the man lurched upright, then swung, coming in again. Digging in his heels, Lance watched as the other telegraphed his roundabout swing. It was a comparatively easy task to dodge that wild swing, to step inside it and hammer two short, sharp blows to the other's throat.

The man gasped for breath, then threw out his arms wildly, caught them around Lance's back, clutching them tightly against his spine, pressing with all of his strength. For the first time Lance glimpsed defeat. The pressure on his back increased as the other exerted all of his strength in an attempt to snap his spine like a rotten twig.

He felt himself being lifted off his feet, and strove with all of his strength to keep his heels on the ground, knowing that once the other lifted him clear, it would be only moments before his back was broken under that terrible strain. The human spine could only give so far and then it was bound to snap. Madly he tried to gulp air down into his heaving, straining lungs. Blackness floated in front of his stultified vision and he felt his consciousness slipping away from him like a wet rag.

For a second the other, as if confident of the outcome now, relaxed his hold slightly. The decrease in pressure lasted only for a fleeting moment, but it was long enough for Lance to jerk his arms free. Without pausing, he thrust the heel of his palm under the other's jaw and pushed with all of his strength.

The other merely grunted and tightened his arms until the pain made Lance dizzy. Again he pushed, but it made no difference to the other. Only one chance left now and Lance took it. Pulling back his arms, he held them wide, straightened his hands and chopped down with a savage blow on the sides of the other's neck. The big man yelled aloud, staggered back, releasing his hold instantly.

It took several moments for Lance to clear his vision. The other had dropped to his knees in the dust, was leaning forward with curious retching noises coming from his heaving throat. Lance waited for him, knowing that there were people on both sides of the street now, and at the windows of the buildings, watching all that was going on. When his opponent finally staggered to his feet, Lance saw for the first time the look of fear in the bigger man's eyes and, as he stepped back a couple of paces, face distorted, it was written all over his broad, bruised features. In that second Lance edged forward, feeling the strength beginning to surge back into his arms and legs, knowing that he had the beating of the other. Then the other turned swiftly, a savage movement, and there was the sudden glitter of sunlight on steel, glancing off the long-bladed knife in the man's hand. The killing fever shone again in his eyes, slitted against the sunlight that was reflected off the dusty street.

This was one dirty trick he ought to have expected and hadn't. The other was still sucking in air as he circled Lance slowly, arms extended. Out of the corner of his eye,

Lance saw his own gunbelt lying in the dust a few yards away. Very cautiously, he began to edge towards it, keeping his gaze deliberately averted from it in case the other guessed his intention.

The man's eyes flickered to the right. Lance saw the look, but understood a fraction of a second too late. As he leapt forward, the other kicked out, his booted foot catching Lance behind the right knee, sending his sprawling forward. He hit the ground hard and for a fraction of a second lay there, half-stunned. Then he glimpsed the killer surging forward, saw the downward swing of the glittering knife and forced himself to move, galvanizing his body into action. The blade struck the ground less than an inch from his body and buried itself in the hard dirt. As the other tried to jerk it loose, Lance twisted on to his back and kicked up with his feet, putting all of his strength into the blow. The sunlight shone directly into his slitted eyes so that it was difficult for him to see the other properly, merely as a vague, blurred shadow. But the blow connected, his heels catching the man on the point of the chin, throwing him backward with a wild cry.

Before he could recover, Lance pushed himself to his feet, swung savagely and smashed a sharp blow with his bunched fist at the man's throat. He uttered a high, thin bleat of agony, gurgling shrilly, clawing at his adam's apple, the knife dropping from suddenly nerveless fingers into the dirt. Before the other could bend and reach for it, Lance had kicked it away among the feet of the watching crowd. Then he was following the other as he backed away, driving short, chopping blows at the man's face. With a harsh, choked curse, the other tried to bring up his knee, failed to connect, and staggered back as another blow took him full in the face.

Then the man was down, shaking his head, trying to push himself up on to his hands and knees, spitting blood from his smashed lips. Lance stood over him, staring down.

'Get up,' he said hoarsely.

The other made no reply, still tried to claw his way upright, a low muttering sound coming from his throat as he fought to get air down into his heaving chest. With an effort, he managed to stagger half upright, swayed there. Lance took his time, then kicked him again on the side of the head. This time the man went down in the dust and did not move. It was all over.

Turning, forcing evenness into his tone, Lance said sharply, addressing the watching crowd: 'It's all over, folks. When he comes round I want him out of town.' He eyed the two men who had ridden up with the big man, saw the look of incredulous amazement written all over their hard, coarse features.

'If I ever see him in town again, I'll come gunning for him,' he said meaningly. 'That goes for you and anybody else from the Lazy K ranch if you want to make trouble here. If you behave yourselves, then you're welcome in Vengeance. If you want to be troublesome, then you'll find trouble waiting for you. Get that?'

The men nodded their heads sullenly. For a moment there was a gleam in the eyes of the nearer man, and his right hand hovered suggestively over the butt of his Colt, but by that time Lance had bent, had buckled on his own gunbelt, and there was a hardness in his tone that matched the look on his face as he gritted:

'Try it if you care to, Mister.'

For a second the gunman stared down at him from the saddle, then slowly eased his hand away, lips twisted into a vicious grin. 'Mebbe the next time we meet, Marshal,' he said thinly.

'I'll be waiting,' grunted Lance. He stepped back on to the boardwalk, then jerked a thumb in the direction of the unconscious man lying in the middle of the street. 'Better pick him up and put his head into the horse trough yonder, then put him back on to his mount and ride out.'

Turning his back on them deliberately, knowing that there would be no trouble from either of the men at that moment, he made his way slowly along the street, back to the sheriff's office, opened the door, still conscious of the stares of the townsfolk on his back, went inside and closed the door behind him. Seating himself in the chair at the back of the desk, he forced the tenseness out of his body, forced his limbs and muscles to relax. There was blood on his face where the man's rock-hard fists had cut through the flesh, jarring against the bone, and one side of his head felt numb.

His chest, too, felt as if it had been stoved in and a sharp pain lanced through his body with every breath he took.

Gingerly, he felt beneath his shirt, probing gently with his fingertips, until he had convinced himself that there were no ribs broken, although some felt bruised. For a long moment he had no sense of time. There was silence out in the street, then, after a timeless interval, he heard the sound of horses moving away and guessed that the three Lazy K men had taken his orders and ridden out of town. No doubt they would ride straight across country to inform Wayne Patten of what had happened in Vengeance.

Sitting back, he opened the drawer at the side of the desk, found a bottle of whiskey and a glass. His hand shook a little as he poured himself out a stiff shot and gulped it down. The raw liquor stung the back of his throat, but went down and stayed down, bringing an expanding sphere of warmth into the pit of his stomach. Again he thought of the anger and the bitter hatred that had triggered his fists a little while earlier and, for the second time that day, he seemed to see himself in a far sharper perspective than ever before, to realize what he really was, and to understand, in some small way, the reasons why he had suddenly changed his mind and taken the job of town marshal. That hard taint of violence which he had strangely denied in himself had felt good out there in the street. He knew now that, besides the anger that was in him and the undoubted capacity for hate, there was also the knowledge that he would kill if he had to, not only to keep himself alive or to get back that which was legally his, as he had when he had shot down Sloan and his two companions, but also to prevent the evil outside the town from creeping into Vengeance.

He took another drink, was settling back in his chair, when there was a sudden step on the boardwalk just outside the door and, a moment later, the door opened and Doc Manly came in. The other looked him over for a second, then placed the black bag he was carrying on top of the desk with a deliberate gesture.

'Figured I'd better come over and see if I was needed here, Marshal,' he said quietly, pulling up the other chair and lowering himself in it. 'I saw most of the fight out there, couldn't make up my mind which of you needed my help most. How are you feeling now?' He threw a swift glance in the direction of the half-empty whiskey bottle.

'Reckon I'm all right, Doc,' Lance said slowly. 'At least, I've got a damned good idea of what I'm up against now.' He rubbed his chin musingly. 'I've been wondering what those bystanders would have done if either of those two *hombres* sitting watching had decided to take a hand and pulled a gun on me.'

'Would they have backed you up, you mean?' Manly shook his head slowly but decisively. 'I'm sure they would-n't have. This town is scared, Marshal; scared to do anything that might antagonize Patten.'

'Then why did Benson offer me this job? Because he figured that I wouldn't last a couple of days? Or does he honestly think I can hold it down – without any real help from the town?'

Instead of answering directly, the other said: 'If you'd asked for my advice at the very beginning, I'd have told you to ride out of town, skirting around the main trail and to keep on riding. That's still what I'd say right now if you were to ask me, but I figure you're not likely to do that.'

'No,' said Lance quietly, 'you're right. Something changed me after that *hombre* challenged me out there.'

'I guessed it might.' Without asking, the doctor leaned over and picked up the whiskey bottle, tilting it to his lips.

He smacked them in satisfaction a moment later as he lowered the bottle, then eyed Lance directly. 'I still reckon I ought to take a look at you, Marshal. You've been hurt, you know.'

Lance knew that it would be useless to argue with the other. He allowed himself to be led over to the basin in the corner of the room, submitting meekly while the other bathed his face and neck, then taped his chest so that the pain was eased and he could stand straight and breathe slowly without too much trouble.

'Reckon that ought to do for the time being,' he said finally, taking up his bag from the top of the desk. He gave Lance a quizzical look. 'Next time some *hombre* like that decides to challenge you, use that gun of yours. It'll be far less painful, believe me.'

He stumped out of the office, closing the door behind him. Standing by the glass window, Lance watched him go, moving across the dusty street to his own office in the narrow alley that led off the main street of the town. Some of the strength had come back into Lance's body, and he drew deep breaths down into his lungs, in an effort to clear his head. The whiskey had helped, but he knew better than to drink any more at the moment. At any time, he knew, Patten might come riding into town at the head of his hired gunslingers, looking for trouble, knowing that he would find it there.

It was late afternoon before Patten made any move and, when he did, it was not the kind of move that Lance had expected. The first indication he had that something out of the ordinary was happening was the quiet hush that seemed to settle quite abruptly over the town. In the heat head of the hot afternoon, with a handful of dust devils spiralling along the quiet street, the sudden stillness might have passed unnoticed to an ordinary man, but almost instantly Lance was on his feet, moving towards the window, peering out into the sunlight.

The saloon keepers were no longer standing at the doors of the saloons. Even across the street at the hotel the usual small knot of men was conspicuously absent, and only two horses were in sight, tethered to the hitching rail outside one of the stores at the far end of the street. Tension seemed to flow in the heated air of afternoon. Thick and heavy, it could be felt, and Lance moved to the door of the office, opening it and stepping out.

His movements were controlled, quick and quiet. He stood waiting, motionless, gun ready in its holster as he stared with narrowed eyes at the dust cloud on the northern edge of town, moving closer along the street. From it emerged the shapes of perhaps a dozen riders, moving their mounts with an ominous slowness along the street, heading in his direction.

Lance's stomach muscles tightened spasmodically and he could feel the nerves along his legs and arms begin to jump a little. These were familiar symptoms that he had known and experienced many times before, always at just such a moment as this, when danger seemed very close and coming nearer with every passing second. He thinned his lips into a tight grin, confident that when the action started up he would be steady enough. Always, in the past, he had been.

The small band of riders reached the saloon, paused there for a moment, then came on, with one man in the lead, a tall, powerfully built man with a hard, craggy face and narrow eyes that stared unwinkingly into Lance's, eyes that were as emotionless as those of a snake.

Wayne Patten.

The other reined his mount in front of the sheriff's office, sat easily in the saddle, not once taking his eyes off Lance. Then he said thinly, very softly: 'Been wanting to meet you, Turner. They tell me that you've taken over the marshal's job here ia Vengeance, after shooting down Sloan.'

'That's right.' Lance spoke evenly. 'They elected me marshal and I took the job. Reckon they decided they needed a man who wasn't crooked.'

If the barb went home, the other gave no sign of it. His

face remained quite unmoved. Only the lines around his eyes and the corners of his mouth seemed to have deepened a shade. Then he nodded. 'At the moment I ain't got no call to argue with you, Marshal.' He paused, then swung himself easily from the saddle, gave a quick nod to the men riding with him, and walked towards Lance.

'Reckon you and I can talk this little matter over in the privacy of your office, Turner,' he said genially. 'Seems it only concerns the two of us. No reason why we shouldn't discuss it calmly, man to man.'

Lance had the feeling that there was more to the other's geniality than showed on the surface, but he nodded slowly and stepped back into the office, opening the door for the other. Outside, the riders from the Lazy K ranch sat their horses in silence, eyes flicking along the street, and their very presence gave Lance a tight feeling in the pit of his stomach.

FOUR

THE WILD BREED

'Now, Marshal, let's you and me get down to business. I'm not a difficult man to get along with, and I'm sure we can come to some agreement.'

Patten lowered himself into the chair opposite Lance and settled his body back comfortably. 'I don't aim to be causing trouble here in Vengeance, but as you can see out there, I've got plenty of men to back up any play I may decide to make, and so far as I can see, there's only you here. Don't be expecting the townsfolk to give you any help.'

'I never figured they would,' said Lance simply. He rolled himself a smoke, eyed the other squarely. 'Just what sort of an agreement are you proposing, Patten?'

The other grinned expansively.

'Well, it's this way, Marshal. I own the Lazy K spread outside of town. It's the biggest spread in this neck of the territory by a long way, and I aim to make it even bigger. But there are some ranchers in the vicinity who won't sell out, even at a fair price. Now I'm only trying to be reasonable here. They can't work their land as I can. They don't have the capital and most of 'em have their ranches mortgaged up to the hilt. The bank in town made most of those loans a few years back, and as I'm the biggest stockholder in the bank, I guess that gives me the right to say when

65

those loans are to be called in and whether or not there's to be any extension on them.' He shrugged his shoulders, chewed on the end of the black cigar he had just lit. 'Most of 'em don't have any security at all. You know how things are in this part of the State, Marshal.'

'I'm afraid I don't,' Lance said evenly. 'Suppose you tell me.'

'It's only human nature, I suppose, to figure that once you've bought your ranch and spread, that's all there is to it.' He shook his head slowly, ponderously, and went on: 'I'm afraid that isn't quite the case. A couple of bad years, a drought maybe, and half your cattle are gone. Then there are rustlers somewhere in the territory who run off with a herd now and again. As far as I'm concerned, a couple of thousand head means little, but these small ranchers could be ruined then.'

'So you've decided that you'll call in most of the loans the bank has made during the past few years, and if any of the ranchers can't pay them back, you'll take over their land and ranches.'

'That's the way you have to do things in business.' The other puffed on his cigar furiously for a moment, blowing smoke towards the ceiling. 'Sheriff Pardee was a good man, but he was inclined to turn a blind eye towards this, reckoned that because a man had a hard time one year, the law ought to be altered in his case. But you can't twist and change the law like that, Marshal.'

'And what happened to Pardee?' murmured Lance, softly. 'I did hear that he was shot down on the street outside this office.'

'Understand now, Marshal,' Patten said quickly, 'I knew nothing of that until it was all over. There was some kind of gunfight in town, and the sheriff just happened to be in the middle of it. As soon as I found out, I deputised some of the boys and went looking for his killer, but he got clean away, probably over the border into Mexico.'

'And Sloan was elected in his place?'

'That's right. A good man in some ways, or so they reckoned.' Patten swivelled suddenly in his chair, his gaze sliding away from Lance's as if afraid to meet it. 'I know that Sheriff Pardee was a man well liked in this town and most of the men here felt strongly about his death. But there was nothing we could do about it. I reckon that's why they didn't like Sloan so much. It wasn't an easy thing to do for a man to step into Pardee's shoes.'

For a moment Lance almost believed the other. Then he said thinly: 'I did hear that it was one of your men who shot down Pardee, Patten. Could be the man who told me that was mistaken.'

Patten tightened his lips, then swung around to stare out of the dusty window, slitting his eyes against the glare of sunlight that streamed into the office.

'First off, you've got to understand how things are in Vengeance,' he said, with a touch of tightness to his voice. 'It don't do to get the wrong idea about this place. They tell me that you've been up in the hills for the last two years, and I reckon you may be out of touch with things. There's been a lot of trouble before between the small ranchers and my own men. There are some nesters about five miles outside of town, trying to make trouble. We don't want 'em here but, just to spite me, the ranchers have been teaming up with these folk, shooting down my men and herding some of my cattle off the range.'

'You got any proof of what you're tellin' me?' Lance demanded harshly.

'Enough for me.' Patten shifted his huge bulk uncomfortably in the swivel chair, rubbing the back of his hand over his chin. 'I had to hire myself some fast men with a gun to protect my own interests.'

'And just where did Sloan come into it? You denyin' that he was in your pay?'

'Certainly I'm denying it.' The surprise in the other's face came quickly under control, as did the sudden surge of anger that showed in his eyes. For a moment the other was silent, obviously trying to decide how to handle the man who faced him, a little unsure of himself. 'If you've been told that, then some *hombre* has been lying to you, Marshal.'

'I'll make up my own mind on that point.'

Lance sat up straight in his chair, drawing on the cigarette, pulling the smoke down into his lungs. He regarded the other thoughtfully for a long moment. 'Right now my only concern is to keep law and order in Vengeance. If you or your men want to ride into town, then you're welcome to do so, but if you start to make trouble here then I'll have to do something about it.'

There was an open sneer on the other's face now and it had darkened a little with barely controlled fury. 'Do you reckon that you can make any trouble for us, Marshal? One man against the men I have?' He shook his head, lips thinned back across his teeth, his face tight.

Lance's eyes, narrowed and cold, held the other's steadily. He controlled his own tight rise of feeling. 'I'm just warning you, Patten. If you reckon that I'll carry out your orders for pay as Sloan did, then you're making a big mistake. I aim to do the job I've been given as I see it, no other way. Mebbe you won't like it; mebbe some of the folk here in Vengeance won't like it. But that's the way it's going to be.'

'Then I guess you're a bigger fool than I took you for, Marshal,' sneered the other. He heaved himself to his feet, stood staring malevolently down at Lance for a long moment, then turned on his heel and stalked out of the office.

Wearily, Lance got to his feet and walked around the edge of the desk to the window, watching the rancher as he strode across the street to where the rest of his men were waiting. He stood talking with one of them for a while, then swung himself up into the saddle, waved his right arm, and rode out of town with all of the men following him except the man he had spoken with a few moments earlier. Lance's eyes narrowed as he saw the man ride his horse towards the saloon, throw a swift glance up and down the street and then dismount, hitching the horse to the rail, and pushing open the batwing doors, going inside.

That there was more trouble brewing was obvious. In the bright sunlight Lance had managed to get a good look at the man Patten had left behind in town. He had been a scrawny man, small and stooped, with legs that were noticeably bowed from long riding in the saddle. His hair had been long and unkempt under the wide-brimmed hat, and the gun rig that he wore proclaimed him to be a professional killer.

Lance stood quietly in the shadows, watching the door of the nearby saloon. At the far end of the street, where the darkness was already closing in on the town, he could see several trail hands who had ridden into town beginning to move towards the other saloon further along the street. Faintly in the distance he could hear the tinkle of a piano and the sound of harsh laughter reached him on the breeze. But there was nothing like that coming from the saloon just across the street from where he stood. Half an hour earlier he had watched several of the more important townsfolk go inside. Benson and the banker had been there, together with most of the storekeepers and the doctor.

At the moment he had no idea why they had collected there in this way, except perhaps to discuss some of the things which had happened during the past twenty-four hours. He grinned wryly to himself as a thought crossed his mind. Maybe, he reflected, they had already come to the decision that it was far too dangerous having a man like him as marshal of Vengeance, antagonizing Patten to the point where it seemed inevitable that the other would come riding into town with his hired killers and take the place apart. If that happened, then not only would Lance Turner suffer, but everyone in the town. Patten would not be keen to hold back his men once they rode in.

He wondered what his reaction would be if they decided to ask him to turn in his badge, telling him that they had changed their mind and had elected a new man to the job of marshal, someone perhaps a little more acceptable to Wayne Patten. Deep down inside, he knew that he ought to hurl the star in their faces and tell them to go to hell, if that was what they wanted, but somehow he knew that he would not do that. He had signed that contract earlier that afternoon, and he meant to stay on in the job until he had finished what he had to do, or until he lay dead and stiff in the dust of the street.

There was a sudden movement in the shadows near the saloon. A man stepped out of the narrow alley that ran alongside the building, came out into the street a couple of dozen yards from where Lance stood. Eyes narrowed, he noticed that it was the gunman Patten had left behind in Vengeance.

The man shouted intemperately: 'You there, Marshal?'

Lance let his gaze rest steadily on the other, but the muscles of his stomach grew tight under his belt. 'You looking for trouble, Mister?'

A second passed. Then there was movement near the doors of the saloon and out of the corner of his eye Lance saw that most of the men inside, hearing the sudden shout, had come crowding forward to see what was going on in the street. Vaguely, he made out the small figure of Benson close up to the doors.

'That was one of my buddies you shot down, Marshal, when you gunned down Sloan.'

'Too bad.'

Lance's tone was even now that he knew the other would not back down until one of them was dead. 'Reckon he ought to have known better than to be in cahoots with a double-dealing lawman like Sloan.'

The gunslinger sidestepped guardedly, edging into the centre of the street, his hands held poised above his guns. His eyes were unblinking, fixed on Lance's face. Here, thought the other, was a gunman who tried to figure out when his opponent meant to draw, watching a man's face for the first sign that he intended to make a move. Lance grinned faintly. He waited, knowing that the waiting would be harder on the other than it was on him.

His eyes narrowed until they were mere slits and he deliberately unfocused his gaze so that everything in the background swam away, out of focus, leaving only the man who faced him, twenty yards away. The other moistened his lips, aware that the townsfolk were watching now, that he had come up against a man who refused to be stampeded into action, who was not afraid of facing him.

Suddenly, as if unable to bear the rising tension any longer, the gunman's hands flashed downward with the speed of a striking snake, but the guns had scarcely cleared their holsters before the twin shots from the long-barrelled Colt in Lance's hand, rock steady in its aim, blasted along the street.

The man staggered back, face twisted into a look of distorted fury and shock as the bullets struck home, smashing both wrists. He yelled loudly, the guns falling from his nerveless fingers.

Purposefully, Lance strode forward. Beside him the doors of the saloon opened and men began to move towards him across the street, their booted heels rattling hollowly on the wooden boardwalk.

Lance's voice was coldly vicious as he stood over the man lying on the ground, hugging both arms to his chest. A low moan from the other's throat, and he looked strangely small and helpless squatting there, rocking back and forth on his haunches as the agony of the smashed wrists lanced through his arms.

'Get on to your feet,' Lance said sharply. 'I'll get the doc to take a look at you, and then you'll be spending the night in jail. Tomorrow we'll decide what we're going to do with you.'

Doctor Manly came forward at Lance's signal, examined the other's wrists, then said quietly: 'I'll have to bandage 'em up, Marshal. Reckon he won't be able to use his hands for a little while.'

'That's what I figgered,' Lance murmured, as he

holstered his gun. 'Do what you can for him, Doc, then I want him over at the jail.'

'You sure that you're doing the right thing, Marshal?' interrupted Benson, stepping hesitantly forward.

Lance whirled to face him. His voice was harsh and tight as he said: 'I know exactly what I'm doing, Mister Benson. You hired me as town marshal, and that's the job I intend to do. This man broke the law when he tried to draw on me. Besides, I don't need any charge to hold him in jail overnight.'

Benson opened his mouth to say something more, then closed it with an audible snap, shrugging helplessly. One of the storekeepers spoke up. 'We been talking things out in the saloon, Marshal. Reckon there's something we got to say to you, but we don't know how to put it. Sure we hired you for the job of marshal, but it seems you've been taking things too much in hand. We didn't aim that you should start shooting up everybody who came riding into town, especially any of Patten's men.'

Lance felt a flame begin to burn at the back of his skull. He held it, controlling it, pushing it back into the far recesses of his mind when it tried to pick out and take over his brain to the exclusion of everything else. There was something here he could guess at but which he could only just begin to understand. These men were afraid. They had brought a lot of this trouble on themselves, but now they saw more trouble brewing for them if they allowed him to have his way, and they wanted to stop it before it was too late.

'And during this talk that you've had,' he said tightly, 'you reckoned that you'd done the wrong thing when you elected me marshal. Is that it?'

'Well,' went on the other hesitantly, 'we know you could do the job properly and that you're as straight and honest a man as we could hope to get for the job, but—'

'But it's the way I'm going about it that you don't like. That's it, isn't it? You want law and order, but none of you is prepared to fight for it. You reckon that it can be got easily and without any trouble. Well, that just isn't so. You've got to fight for law and order. That's the only way you'll ever get it. And I reckon we'd better get one thing straight right now.' He turned his head very slowly, letting his gaze pass over each one of them in turn. 'I mean to stay in this job until I've finished what I set out to do. And if that means shooting down every one of Patten's men who makes trouble, or putting 'em in jail, then I'll do it.'

He sensed the hostility in their minds as they stared at him in the darkness, but knew that their spirit was broken for the time being, that they would not argue with him. There came a time, he reflected, when a man had to live or die according to what he found in himself. But first he had to plumb the bottom-most depths in his own self, to use the good that was within him to its best advantage, without letting the evil which went hand in hand with the good take over and use him. He knew that he had reached that time. He had to keep himself cold and clear in his mind, to go through with what he had to do. Turning, he saw that the doctor had taken out the bandages from his bag and had almost finished tying up the other's wrists. He gave a quick nod.

'When you've finished, Doc,' he said quietly.

Manly paused, then went on with his work. Lance wondered whether the other agreed with the decisions that the rest of the townsfolk had apparently reached in the saloon. When he had first spoken with the other, he had seemed determined to help in driving out the evil that existed around the town, and that he did not really care how it was done.

'All right,' Lance spoke up as the doctor stepped back from the injured man. 'Let's get over to the jailhouse.'

'You ain't going to hold me for long, Marshal,' said the gunman sneeringly. 'When Patten hears about this night's work, he'll come riding into town and then neither you nor any of these folk here will be alive to know what happens later.'

'We'll see about that when he comes,' murmured

Lance evenly. 'In the meantime I've got a cell waiting for you.'

The man walked swiftly, angrily, along the street, staring neither to right nor left. Behind them the saloon began to empty of its occupants as the townsfolk made their way back to their homes. The street was silent in the darkness.

Pausing outside the sheriff's office, Lance said sharply: 'Open the door and go on in.'

The other turned his head.

'How in hell do you expect me to open the door like this?' he gritted.

Cautiously, still alert for any trick, Lance circled around the other, his hand near the gun in his belt, then twisted the handle and kicked the door open, nodding to the other to step inside. He followed close on the man's heels, kicked the door shut behind him, then, keeping one wary eye on the gunslinger, lit one of the lamps on the desk and motioned the other towards the passageway leading to the cells at the rear of the building.

Their footsteps echoed hollowly along the walls as they walked to the back of the building. Unlocking one of the cell doors, Lance stood on one side as the other entered, then slammed the door and locked it. Through the bars he saw that the other had stretched himself out on the low bunk, was staring at him with slitted malevolent eyes, vitriolic in their hatred.

Maybe, he thought, as he walked back into the outer office, it would have been better if he had killed the man instead of just wounding him. It was still difficult for him to realize why he had done that, why he had not shot to kill. Certainly the idea of letting the gunslinger live once he had drawn on him had not been in his mind a split second before he had squeezed the trigger of the Colt.

Opening the street door, he stepped out on to the boardwalk for a breath of cool air, drawing it down into his lungs. Slowly the tension in him began to ease a little and the mind which he had locked against thought opened again and he found a strange sense of relief in his brain.

He rolled himself a smoke, lit the cigarette and stood there, leaning his shoulders against the side of the building, letting his gaze drift along the street.

This could be a good town in which to live if it were not for the violence that gripped it; the greed and avarice in the men who attempted to control it, who sought to rule the lives of all who lived there. No man could live in peace under those conditions, he told himself. Someone had to make the place fit for honest people to live in. If he didn't do it, then there was no telling when they would get anyone to carry out the task. It was not going to be an easy thing to do, and even now he was not sure of his ability to do it alone. Yet there was no one in town who seemed ready to back him up. Maybe Patten had been right. What chance did one man have against an army of hired killers with orders to shoot him down on sight? Even in town there were many shadows where a would-be killer might be hiding at that very moment, ready to gun him down from cover.

He smoked for several minutes, aware that the glowing tip of the cigarette gave away his position, made him a target for any bullet from the shadows. But he also knew that he was being watched by the people of Vengeance, that they were waiting for the moment when he would break under the strain.

In spite of the tension in him, he slept well that night, woke to find dawn streaking the eastern sky with grey. He washed and shaved, felt better, then walked over to the hotel room for breakfast.

Seating himself at the table near the window, where he could watch all that happened out on the street, he chewed slowly and ruminatively at his food. He ate bacon, oat scones and beans, finishing them off with strong, black coffee which burned the back of his throat, but brought a pleasant warmth into his bones.

He was on the point of getting to his feet when a light step nearby caused him to glance up. She was a tall girl, her hair dark and braided, and the braids were coiled on her shoulders and around her head. Her eyes were resting on him appraisingly, as if trying to gauge what kind of a man he really was, and her lips were pressed firmly together. She wasn't a saloon girl, that much was obvious from the start.

'May I have a word with you, Marshal?' she asked, her voice low and pleasant.

A little self-consciously, he got to his feet, looking across at her. Her head, he noticed, came well above the level of his shoulder. 'Certainly, Ma'am.' He nodded towards the other chair. 'Won't you sit down and tell me what's on your mind?'

Gracefully she lowered herself into the chair, peeled off the long black gloves and laid them on the table in front of her. There was an odd expression on her face as if she were trying to make up her mind whether or not she was doing the right thing.

'You're probably wondering who I am and what a woman like me would want with the Marshal so early in the morning.' There was a coolness in her voice that he found oddly disturbing. 'My name is Grace Pardee. I think you knew my father?'

'Why yes. I didn't know him too well. But I—'

There was a sharp intensity in her voice that surprised him as she leaned forward and went on: 'I've waited all these years to avenge his death. I saw you last night when you took that gunman into jail. You don't look the kind of man who would run away from trouble. That's why I came to see you. Not because you're the Marshal and responsible for upholding the law, but because I think you're the only man in town who will see to it that justice is done and that my father's killer is brought to justice and tried for his murder.'

'I think I understand.' Lance nodded. 'Do you know who killed him?'

'I only know that Patten ordered his death. If he wasn't the man who pulled the trigger, he's just as guilty as anyone.'

'So you want me to arrest Patten and charge him with your father's murder?'

'Yes.'

He shrugged.

'I'm afraid that it isn't as easy as that, Miss Pardee. I've got to have evidence to convince a jury and—'

Her voice was thin, her lips curled into a disdainful smile, as she broke in: 'Convince a jury, Marshal? You must be joking. Where would you get a jury here in Vengeance who would dare to convict a man like Patten, even if you had all the evidence you needed?'

'So what do you want me to do?'

'Go after Patten and kill him.'

He stared at her in sudden surprise, then pursed his lips into a hard line. 'Until he steps outside of the law, there ain't a thing I can do, Miss Pardee,' he said quietly. 'Once he breaks the law, then I'll go after him.'

'Then you're not only a fool but you're a dead man.' For a moment longer she sat there, then drew on her gloves and pushed back her chair, getting to her feet. 'I thought you would help me,' she murmured flatly. 'I see that I was mistaken. Patten is going to get off scott free with another murder. I wonder how long you're going to stay alive, Marshal? Perhaps not as long as any of the others.'

She walked away a few paces, then turned, and there was a curious note in her voice as she said: 'As for that gunman you've got locked up in jail, he won't be there after midday. Already Benson and the others are signing a paper for his release. Seems that Patten has already got word through to them. They're scared for their lives, like everyone else in this god-forsaken town.'

Lance thought he detected tears in her eyes as she turned sharply and stumbled out of the room. For a moment he wanted to get to his feet and hurry after her, to tell her that he would do as she had asked, but deep down inside he knew that would be impossible, and he forced himself to remain where he was, watching through the window as she hurried away along the boardwalk, not once looking round for him to see that she was crying.

He finished his coffee, setting the cup down in front of him, then got up and walked quickly across the street to the lawyer's office. Rapping sharply on the door, he waited impatiently until he heard the shuffling footsteps on the other side and, a moment later, the door creaked open. Benson peered out, blinking his eyes against the red rays of the rising sun that flooded into the alley.

'Oh, it's you, Marshal,' he said, shifting himself uncomfortably from one foot to the other.

'That's right, Benson.' Lance moved forward. 'I'd like to have a talk with you if I may.'

'Right now?' inquired the other.

Lance gave a vigorous nod.

'Right away,' he affirmed. 'It's important.'

'Very well. Come inside.'

The other stood on one side to allow Lance to enter, then closed the door of the musty office behind him.

'What's on your mind, Marshal?'

'I've just had an interesting talk with Miss Pardee.'

'Sheriff Pardee's daughter.' Benson gave a quick, bird-like nod. 'She was pretty badly cut up when her father was killed. I don't reckon she ever got over it.'

'She told me some very interestin' things, particularly about this *hombre* I locked in jail last night. Told me that you'd signed a paper setting him free.'

'She had no right to go spilling things like that around town,' said the other with a trace of righteous anger in his voice.

'I reckon that she had the right to tell me,' said Lance grimly. 'Seems that nobody else was going to. I reckon I was supposed to be the last person in town to know.'

'Now don't take it that way, Marshal,' protested the other. 'You know as well as I do that we got no call to hold him any longer unless you bring a charge against him; and I don't see what you can charge him with. Disturbing the peace, maybe, but that'll only get him a fine, and you can bet that Patten will pay that like a shot just to get him out of jail. There's a lot of sense in doing things our way, believe me.'

'I'm trying to believe you,' went on Lance harshly. 'But at the moment I'm finding it mighty difficult. Seems to me that you've changed your ideas right around since you asked me to take on the marshal's job. Could be you've had second thoughts about it and figure I'm not the best man for the job. Could be that Patten has given you only so much time to get rid of me or he'll ride into town and bust this place wide open. Is that what you're so scared about?'

'I've got to consider what's best for the town,' said the other defensively. 'When I asked you to be Marshal, I figured that a man as fast as you were with a gun would be just the kind we needed here. Somebody who wouldn't take Patten's side and who could be relied on to fight no matter what the odds. Now I'm not so sure about you.' The other's eyes avoided him.

'But I'm sure about you,' Lance told him. 'I reckoned I might get a little support as Marshal from the citizens of Vengeance. Seems I was wrong. Ain't nobody here I could swear in as a deputy and rely on him to back me up.'

'Knowing Patten, did you expect anybody to back you up?'

'I thought that the least I could expect was for you to back me whenever I put one of these killers in jail, where he belongs.'

Benson was silent, staring down at the floor under his feet. He did not look up for several moments, the red sunlight, streaming in through the dusty window, touching his face with a red glow, throwing the planes of his features into shadow.

'All right,' he murmured slowly, feebly. 'Maybe you're right about us. But I've signed that paper now and I can't go back on it. We've got to set this man free.'

'Even though he tried to kill me last night?'

'Even so. Besides, with those smashed wrists of his, he

won't be any trouble to anybody for a long time to come.'

Lance waited for a long moment, forcing down the anger in his mind. Then he gave a sharp nod of his head and walked out of the room. He had the feeling that he needed the smell of clean, pure air in his nostrils after being in that room with the other. But even out on the boardwalk there was a foul taste in his mouth.

Fifteen minutes later, when he approached the jail, he found a small deputation of men waiting for him. Benson was there, as he had expected, with Manly and several of the others.

'Are you in on this deal, too, Doctor?' Lance asked sarcastically.

Manly shook his head emphatically.

'I've been against it from the start, Marshal,' he said, staring contemptuously at the others. 'But it seems I've been outvoted. I reckon they gave you a free hand to clean up this town and to get rid of Patten in the process. They don't seem to have done that.'

'Now just try to see our point of view,' butted in one of the storekeepers, but before he could go on, Benson said harshly: 'We're here to enforce this order that we've made. Better open up that cell and let him out, Marshal.'

For a moment Lance debated whether or not to refuse to obey, then he shrugged his shoulders resignedly. The deep-seated anger was still in him, bubbling up swiftly in an attempt to engulf him utterly. But he still managed to hold it in check.

'Very well, if that's the way you want it,' he grated hoarsely. Stepping inside, he led the way along the passage to the cell, unlocked the door and brought the gunman out with a savage jerk of his thumb.

There was a sneering grin on the man's face as he stepped past Lance and, for an instant, his eyes slitted. 'Reckoned you couldn't hold me, Marshal,' he said, tightly. 'Seems these folk here have a mite more sense than you have.'

'I wouldn't be too sure of that,' Lance muttered thinly.

'The next time I see you in Vengeance I'll shoot to kill. Just remember that.'

The man brushed past him, out into the outer office. Turning, Lance whirled on the men around him, forced Benson to meet his harsh, savage gaze. 'I suppose you know what you're doing, letting a killer like that go free. Do you reckon that's going to stop Patten riding into town and shootin' the place up? Do you?'

He saw the involuntary stiffening of Benson's back as the other pulled himself up to his full height, and he smiled a little. The wariness in his mind was even sharper now, a tightening in his chest, and he knew better than to ignore it. The fear in these men was perhaps natural – but not their attempt to hide it behind a veil of trying to do the right thing.

For a second Benson seemed on the point of saying something in his own defence, then he let his gaze slide away, turned on his heel and marched along the corridor after the others.

Was it right of him to blame these men for what they had done? Lance wondered wearily. Each man had to fight according to his own lights, and none of these men would be able to handle a gun like those out on the Lazy K ranch. Perhaps they had figured he would fit in where Sloan left off if they elected him marshal, perhaps they reckoned he might step down when the going got tough.

FIVE

THE NESTERS

Lance stayed in the office all morning. Outside, the street filled with clouds of dust as riders came and went, their mounts churning up the yellow, acrid grains. The sun lifted to its zenith at high noon and a heat pressure lay like the flat of some gigantic hand over the town. So far there had been no trouble from Patten. The killer that Lance had shot up the previous night had ridden out of town the minute he had been released from jail. No doubt Patten was building up a plan against Lance, but at the moment there was nothing to tell him what it might be.

He ate a hurried meal that afternoon in the hotel room overlooking the street, turning things over in his mind. There were so many loose ends in this town and at the moment he could see no way of tying them all together. Just where did Grace Pardee fit into it all? A girl filled with a terrible sense of revenge, seeking someone to help her destroy her father's killer. He wondered how many other men she had approached, asking them to ride out and kill Patten; for there seemed to be not the slightest doubt in her mind that it had been Wayne Patten who had ordered her father's slaying.

He drank his coffee slowly, chewing on that thought. Perhaps she was right, he decided finally. Whoever had ridden into town with orders to shoot down Pardee, he really meant little. He had been nothing more than a gun. You pointed him and he shot; that was all. He probably did not even know Pardee. It was the man who gave the orders, the man who really pulled the trigger, who had been the real murderer.

For a moment, sitting there, he fingered the silver star on his shirt, turning it in his fingers so that it flashed brilliantly in the sunlight. All at once the hostility of these people did not mean anything. He was outside of them all. He knew now how Sheriff Pardee must have felt at times. A lawman had to be above the ordinary everyday life of the town. He ran the back of his hand over his brow. The hotel room still held the intense heat and dust of the day, even though the windows had been opened.

Getting roughly to his feet, he started for the door, had almost reached it, when the clerk came in, saw him and walked across. He held out a note to Lance.

'This came for you five minutes ago, Marshal,' he said tightly.

Lance took it, waited until the other had gone, then opened it and read through it quickly. There were two lines of scrawling, ragged writing on it, some of the words so badly written that it was only with difficulty that he succeeded in making them out.

I got to see you right away, Marshal, along the alley past Benson's place, on the edge of town. I'll be waiting there for you.

There was no signature and Lance turned it over several times in his fingers. It could be a trap, in all probability it was, but there was something about it which made him realize that he would have to go, whether there was an ambush laid there for him or not. A swift glance as he made his way out of the hotel told him that the clerk was not in his usual position behind the desk. That could mean anything, of course. His eyes narrowed a little as he touched the Colt at his side, then stepped out into the hot sunlight, the sharp stench of the dust at the back of his nostrils.

Stepping off the boardwalk of the main street into the narrow alley that stretched away to the edge of town to the east, he let his gaze wander about him sharply, taking in everything that lay in front of him. The houses here were squat and unlovely, crowded together so that they stood side to side with no space between them. In a way that helped. It meant there were fewer places in which a would-be killer might be crouched, waiting to draw a bead on him and shoot him down from ambush. But the tightness of tension was still in his chest as he made his way cautiously forward, keeping in the exact middle of the alley.

The alley was quiet, too quiet for his liking. He was like an animal now. The knowledge that there might be danger lying in wait for him had sharpened his senses until they were far keener than before. Nearby there was a stinking yard where hides had been stretched out on wooden racks to dry in the sun and, further along, were warehouses where the stores in the town were kept. On the left he noticed Benson's office. The door was shut and nothing moved behind the glass windows. Gently he eased the Colt up and down in the leather holster. On the face of things, it was almost as if the street had gone to sleep. Here, he felt sure, was where it would happen if that letter had been a ruse to get him out into the open.

Every nerve and muscle tense in his body, he walked forward very slowly, one foot directly in front of the other, his keen-eyed gaze flicking slowly from side to side, every limb poised to hurl himself to either side if trouble should start up without warning. The empty, tight feeling in his stomach and chest increased.

Still no sound, no movement, in any direction. From behind him a moment later there was the dull sound of hooves on the hard-packed dirt of the main street, but the rider did not turn into the alley. Lance let his breath out in a long sigh, and continued to walk along the alley.

He had almost reached the end, in front of him the alley formed a narrow trail that struck due east into rough country half a mile further on, when a sharp hiss from one of the tumble-down buildings caused him to whirl quickly, hand dropping towards the gun.

'Don't shoot, Marshal. It's only me.'

Carefully Lance made his way forward, then found himself staring down into the face of the old man he had rescued from the blazing ranch house that night when he had ridden out of town, hoping to escape from the place.

'Herb Keene,' he said harshly. 'Did you send that note for me?'

'Sure did,' affirmed the other. 'You look surprised, Marshal.'

'I am a little. Why should you want to see me and so secretly?'

'You know why they hate you so much in Vengeance, Marshal?' There was a sly humour on the old man's face as he glanced up, squinting against the glare of the sunlight. 'They know that what you're doing is right, and they know that if you only had the chance you could break Patten and his hired killers, that you could clean up this town.'

'Then why are they trying to get rid of me?' Lance demanded.

'They're scared that when the showdown comes some of them are going to find themselves in the middle of a ruckus with a gunfight blazing around 'em,' said the other with a touch of impatience. 'This town is wide open for something like that. They can see it comin', but they want to try to hold it off as long as they can.'

'And where do you fit into it?' Lance wanted to know.

Frowning, the other glanced furtively along the street in both directions, moistening his lips. 'I got friends who might be prepared to help you, Marshal. Men who can handle guns if they have to.'

Lance stared at the other in surprise. This was the last thing he had expected from Keene. When he had seen the other first he had been hemmed in the ruins of his own ranch house, surrounded by a bunch of Patten's gunslingers, fighting a losing battle for his life. Now here he was, claiming that he was in a position to help him.

'These friends of yours,' Lance began. 'Who are they? Why should they want to help me against Patten?' Suspicion lay in his tone.

'You forgotten what it is that Patten really wants, Marshal? Not the town, he could ride in and take it over whenever he likes. He wants the land around Vengeance and to get that he has to get rid of the small ranchers like me. So far they've been too busy looking out fer themselves, but I reckon it might be possible to talk 'em into banding together against Patten if there's a showdown coming. And then there are the nesters. They've got a grudge against Patten. He's tried to run 'em off their land, sworn out affidavits that they've been rustling his beef, even tried to get the rest of us to believe it.'

'And you reckon they might help me fight Patten? He's a big man and he has plenty of guns to back him up.'

'I guess they'll fight if you'll talk to 'em, Marshal. While Sloan was sheriff in town, they knew they didn't stand a chance. He was in cahoots with Patten and did as he was told. You're different. I guess we all know that now. If you don't get any help from Benson and that crowd, you've got no choice but to fall in with us.'

'Where can I meet 'em? And when?' Lance reached a sudden decision. At the present time he needed every bit of help that he could get. Patten was not going to hold off much longer. Even now he might be rounding up his gunhawks, preparing to ride down into Vengeance.

'Tonight. We'll meet at Diego's place, about seven miles out of town. I'll take you there myself.'

'You sure that you're in a fit state to travel?' Lance glanced at the old man in surprise.

Keene nodded. 'I'll make it,' he said, with a trace of grim determination to his voice. 'I got a score to settle with Patten, too. Takes more than a bullet to stop me.'

*

Twilight came on from the east, lingered briefly, then gave way to dark. Lance saddled up the sorrel in front of the sheriff's office, eased the cinch a shade, then swung up into the saddle, sat easily for a moment, feeling the cool night breeze flow along the street against his body. He sucked in a deep breath of it, feeling it clean and sharp on his tongue. Then he swung out along the dark street, aware of the curious stares of the people as he rode. Keene was waiting for him on the edge of town, where he had promised to be. He sat astride an old mount that stood with its head bowed between its knees.

'We got quite a way to ride, Marshal,' greeted the other. He gigged his mount and they rode out of town, out into the shallows where the creek rippled loudly over the smooth stones, then into the rocky ground that lay beyond, the trail winding and twisting through lava and rough-hewn boulders.

'You're sure that Patten ain't got wind of this meeting you've called?' Lance asked softly.

'Don't reckon so. If he has, then he's keeping mighty quiet about it. I figured he'd have been in town before now, coming to gun you down. Reckon he's had second thoughts on that score.'

Lance tightened his lips in the darkness. Somehow, he doubted that. Patten was not a man who scared easily and, on the face of it, there was not the slightest reason why he should with all of those armed killers at his back. No, Patten had some other reason for not riding into town and carrying out his threat to rid Vengeance of this upstart marshal who refused to knuckle under and take orders from him.

They were a couple of miles in the hills when Lance's sharp ears picked out the muffled sound of other riders in the distance. Swiftly, instinctively, he reined the sorrel, reached out and caught at the other bridle, pulling Keene close to him, his voice cutting urgently through the darkness.

'Keep still! Somebody heading along the trail this way!'

He glimpsed the other's body stiffen in the saddle, then Keene had bent forward a little and there was the faint whisper of sound as the ancient Winchester rasped from its scabbard.

'Hold it there,' Lance whispered. 'We don't want to give ourselves away by shooting at 'em if we can help it. Turn your horse off the trail into the rocks.'

Gently he urged the sorrel forward, cut off the narrow trail, into the upthrusting boulders. Moments later Keene joined him and they slipped from the saddle, dropping out of sight among the rocks that overlooked the trail. The sound of the approaching riders grew louder in their ears. Whoever they were, they were in a hurry, pushing their mounts to the limit. Someone from town, perhaps, who had heard of this meeting by some means and was riding out to warn Patten? It was possible, Lance reflected tightly. If that were the case, then he had a problem on his mind. Whether to stop them or let them go through and trust to his own luck that Patten would be unable to do anything about the meeting until it was too late.

He caught at the man's arm beside him, pulled him down further into the shadow of the boulders. The men were less than a quarter of a mile away now and coming up fast. They went past a couple of minutes later at a punishing pace. Screwing up his eyes, Lance saw that there were four of them, dark shapes crouched low in the saddles. For a moment he wondered if those men had been trailing Keene and himself. If so, then surely their own dust wake would have given the riders warning that they had turned off the trail somewhere. But as he got slowly to his feet he heard the thunder of hooves on the trail, a steady and continuous abrasion of the night, fading swiftly into the distance.

'Who do you reckon they might have been?' murmured the other harshly. He followed Lance to where their mounts stood further back against a solid, rising wall of rock. Carefully, he slipped the rifle back into its leather scabbard, then eased himself into the saddle, face tightening just a shade as pain lanced through his injured shoulder.

'I wish I knew.' Lance mounted up, caught up the reins in his right hand. 'I've a feeling in my bones they're riding out to warn Patten. Didn't recognize any of 'em, did you?'

'Nope. Too dark to see their faces. But I reckon they weren't any of the townsfolk. None of 'em would be riding out in the hills like that at this time of night.'

'Wherever they were going, they seemed in a mighty hurry.'

Lance nodded. His mount picked its way gingerly back to the trail, moving over the rocks that lay scattered on the edge of the hard-packed earth. A little while later they crossed a second narrow trail that angled from their right, cutting across the other and then sweeping round to the north-east.

Dust stayed with them, sharp in their nostrils, to indicate that the men who had passed them earlier had taken that trail and were still ahead of them, probably many miles distant. The silence of the hills that closed about them was not quite absolute. There were faint night sounds in the distance in every direction, and he had the impression of men criss-crossing in the hills and down below on the vast stretching plain that lay to the east of Vengeance. Midnight brought them out to the mouth of a tall, narrow canyon, the sandstone walls rising up to the star-studded heavens. By now a moon had risen, yellow and round, in the east, and there was more than enough light for them to be able to see by.

The horses took their own time here, refusing to be pushed by their riders, their shoes striking the hard rocky ground metallically. Lance could feel the strange pressure of the canyon walls, boxing them in, and gigged his mount with the tips of the spurs, raking them along the sorrel's flanks. The animal bounded forward for a while, then dropped back into its slower gait.

By the time they came out into the open again they

were dropping down out of the hills, and the prairie lay spread out in front of them, bathed in a yellow wash of moonlight. Through slitted eyes Lance was just able to make out the dark shape of a ranch house and a couple of barns in the distance, perhaps a mile away. Swinging right, Keene took the narrow pathway down the hillside that led in the direction of the ranch. Here there was no smell of dust in the air, and Lance knew that the men they had followed for most of the way had somewhere swung off the trail. If they had been Patten's men, he doubted if they would have ridden on to the ranch, not just the four of them.

Keene said: 'That's the place, Marshal. Most of the others ought to be there by now.'

'I don't see any sign of their horses,' Lance said, pointedly. He jerked a thumb in the direction of the fenced-in corral.

'They'll have driven them into one of the barns,' said the other laconically. 'We don't want to advertise the fact that there are plenty of men gathered here. Not if any of Patten's men are on the prowl.'

They reached level ground, passed through a narrow belt of timber, then out on to a broad strip of ground that led up to the ranch. Out of the corner of his eye Lance noticed that the place had been fenced off but that in one place the wire had clearly been trampled down and had not yet been repaired. Some more of Patten's work? he wondered briefly.

But there was no time to consider that point any further. Already they were riding into the courtyard which faced the house, and as if they had been heard, the door opened and a man stood for a fraction of a second silhouetted against the yellow glow from inside, peering out at them. He must have realized a second later that he presented an excellent target to anyone out there who might have come from Patten for he stepped swiftly to one side, then walked forward.

'Keene?' A voice said softly, out of the darkness.

'Yeah, it's me, Diego,' answered the old man. He slipped from the saddle. 'I brought the Marshal along with me. He's interested in hearing what you're going to discuss.'

'Glad to have you with us, Marshal,' murmured the other, extending his hand. He shook Lance's, then gestured towards the barn. 'Reckon you'd better put your mounts with the others, just in case there are any coyotes prowling around tonight. If Patten should get wind of this he'll come riding out hell for leather and he'll bring as many men as he can with him.'

Lance stabled his mount in the long barn, then followed the other two back to the house, going up on to the porch and then into the warm yellow glow from the paraffin lamp. There were a dozen or so men in the large room when Lance went inside, slitting his eyes to adjust them to the brightness of the lamps on the long table. They looked competent and determined men, and each wore a gun low on his hip. Men who might be relied upon to stand up to the might of Wayne Patten? Perhaps, he thought, casting about him, watching their faces closely. If they figured that the reward justified the price they might have to pay.

'This is Marshal Turner,' said Diego quietly. He nodded in Lance's direction. 'Could be that one or two of you have heard of what he's done in Vengeance while he's been Marshal there.'

A few of the men murmured something and nodded their heads. Others merely watched Lance closely from under lowered lids.

Keene spoke up from near the door. 'I reckon we all know why we're here tonight,' he said thinly. 'Patten is trying to drive us off the range. So far he's forced out Sanderson and Williams, and a couple of nights ago he tried after me. Reckon he would have succeeded, too, if it hadn't been for the marshal. He killed three of the varmints and then dragged me out of the ruins.'

One of the men stepped forward. He was a solid shape,

his face burned a dark brown by the weather, by long hours in the saddle, riding the high hills and wide prairie. He was a hard one, Lance thought, watching him, scarred here and there by trouble. Lance had seen many men like him at one time or another in the past, restless and narrow of mind, unless like this one they managed to settle down somewhere before they fell foul of the law and ended up in prison or strung on the end of a rope.

'You reckon, Marshal, that we stand any chance at all against Patten? There are only about a dozen of us, and he has more than fifty men at the ranch toting guns.'

'I thought there were more men.' Lance turned towards Keene, eyed him closely and inquiringly.

'You mean the nesters?' grated the man who faced him. He shook his head and there was something ugly in the sudden twist of his mouth. 'I for one want no help from them. As soon as we get rid of Patten, they'll turn on us like wolves. They came riding here with their Conestoga wagons, putting up their barbed wire fences, hemming us in on the range. We need these open spaces for our cattle, not so that the squatters can fence it up for their crops.'

'I reckon that if you don't throw in your lot with the nesters, then none of you is going to have any cattle left. Patten's your enemy right now. Get rid of him, and I figure we can make a deal with the nesters.'

'You'll never be able to make a deal with them,' declared the man hotly. His eyes narrowed and a spot of colour burned in each cheek. 'There are too many of them moving in from the east. Pretty soon, whether we like it or not, the place will be swarming with 'em like locusts, and there'll be no place left for honest cattlemen.'

'Until that time comes, you've got to decide whether you want to live with men like Patten, or whether you're willing to fight to rid the range of his evil kind.'

'I say we fight,' broke in Keene. 'We got no other choice. Patten's too strong for any of us to think we could go against him single-handed, even with the men we've got. We have to band together. If we do that, then we have a chance.'

The other man grunted something in a low voice, then stepped back into the ranks of men at the end of the room. Diego said, in a smooth tone: 'How do you figure we ought to go about it, Marshal? Seems to me you've had more dealing with this than we have.'

'There's only one way. We've got to hit him before he realizes what is happening.'

'How do we do that?'

'Either we ride out and attack the Lazy K – or we wait until he comes to us and hit him somewhere along the trail.'

'I got me some dynamite,' broke in another man, quietly.

Lance turned to face him, curious. 'Dynamite! Where'd you get that?'

'Had it since the time the railroad did some blasting in the mountains to the west. There ain't much, but I reckon if we was to lay it alongside the trail and draw 'em into it, we might be able to cut their numbers down more to our size.'

Lance gave a quick nod. That was something worth remembering. It was more than he had expected. With high explosive in their hands, it could help to even things up a little.

'Anybody know how Patten managed to get in here and build up such a spread for himself?' he asked after a pause, looking round at the others. 'When I left Vengeance a couple of years before I'd never heard of him.'

'He bought over the old Carruth spread just about the time you must have pulled out,' said Diego. 'He told everyone he'd saved some money from the war and that he had a hankering to settle down here near Vengeance. Shortly after that there was a lot of rustling took place. Everybody lost cattle.'

'Including Patten?'

'Waal, he said he did. Nobody could prove anything, though, because nobody ever got on to his spread to take a look-see. But it was soon obvious that he was sending plenty of head to market in Kansas and Missouri. Then he started to take an interest in the town, got himself elected on to the board of the bank, and, since he had the biggest deposit there, it was only natural that he should back most of the loans the bank made to us smaller men. There was a bad year, drought and fever hit most ranches and we were forced to increase our loans. Then, shortly before you rode into town, Patten started to call in the loans. He wouldn't give any extension this time, said that if we didn't pay up he'd take over our ranches and spreads legal like.'

Lance nodded.

'And of course, very few of you could pay.'

'None of us could. He'd seemed so goddarned friendly at first, telling us that all he wanted to do was help us make our ranches pay and, above all, he was trying to keep the nesters out of the territory. That was what we wanted at the time. The sodbusters have caused nothing but trouble for cattlemen all the way across the state. So we figured he was on our side. Then we saw what his plan really was.'

'He wanted to take over the whole territory, make himself the kingpin.'

'That's right,' agreed the other harshly. 'He only wanted to use us in the beginning.'

'And nobody could prove anything about those cattle that were rustled from your herds?'

'We reckon that Sloan might have been in on that deal, but he ain't going to tell us anything now.'

'Could be that Benson might know something about it,' suggested Keene.

Lance stared at him sharply. 'Any reason why he should?'

'Well, he'd have to make over the deeds for the ranches and the land when those loans were made. Stands to reason he might know something about how Patten got his money.'

'Afraid that wouldn't prove anything,' Lance told him
quietly. 'Patten could have sold those cattle of yours out
east, always assuming he was behind the rustling. You can
be sure he would have covered his trail well if he had been
doing anything like that.'

'Then we don't have anything on him, we can't
even—'

A man outside yelled, long and full, and immediately
afterward there came a loud knocking on the outer door.
Diego got to his feet and went out of the room. Lance,
standing near the window, felt a sudden surge of apprehension in his chest, the feeling that something was
wrong, that while they had been there talking this thing
over, Patten had not waited, but had been doing something.

Diego came back ten seconds later, his face tight and
grim. He signalled to the other men in the room.

'Kemper here has just ridden back from the herd,' he
said, with a thin edge to his tone. 'The men up there were
attacked by a bunch of riders fifteen minutes ago. He says
they may have been Patten's men, but he isn't sure.'

'Then what the hell are we waiting for?' growled Keene.
In spite of his age and his injured shoulder, he was already
half out of the room, moving with the agility of a man half
his age.

There was no stopping the men now. Lance realized
that this latest move had made up their minds for them.
There was a slight weariness in his body as he turned and
followed them out of the room, out of the ranch house
and into the wide courtyard. Already most of the men had
saddled up, were riding their mounts from the barn. He
hurried inside, found the sorrel and tightened the cinch a
little before mounting. His hand wrenched the horse's
head around, spurred heels dug deeply into the beast's
flanks. A leap that covered twelve feet carried him clear of
the wide entrance to the building, then he had swung in
with the others and they were spurring their mounts along
the trail, tightly bunched, leaping over the spot where the

fencing had been trampled down, then swinging along the wide trail that branched towards the north.

For most of the way the men rode in silence, keeping their thoughts to themselves. If they paused to think of what might lie ahead for them, they gave no outward sign. Inwardly, Lance wondered if they were doing the right thing, riding out like this, leaving the ranch totally unprotected for any of Patten's men to come riding in and destroy. Or it might be that those men up there, rustling some of the herd, were only a small part of the force that was waiting for them, waiting to shoot them down along the trail before they were aware of the danger.

But he knew that it would be impossible to stop these men now. A deep and bitter fury drove them on. All they thought of now was to destroy Patten and any of his men they could find. Perhaps a mile further on they heard the sound of shots bucketing through the night. Diego gave a loud yell, kicked at his horse's flanks and leapt ahead of the others. His gun was out and a moment later he fired off a couple of shots into the air. Lance swung in his saddle, pushing his gaze through the darkness. There were clouds covering the moon now and only a vague yellowish glow to indicate where it was.

Then a steer lifted a long, low, mournful protest to the heavens and they were in the open, circling around the milling edge of the herd. Through narrowed eyes, Lance caught a glimpse of the flashes of gunfire from the further rim of the herd, saw the wide-scattered bunch of men riding them down, seeking to cut off a mass of cattle from the main drag and move it out in the direction of the low hills that lay like a black mass of shadow on the horizon. 'Over there!'

Diego gave another high-pierced yell. He wheeled his mount, sent it leaping over the flat ground. Lance rode swiftly past a bunch of longhorn cattle, crouched low in the saddle. Rain began to drip from the low clouds, but he scarcely noticed it. From directly ahead of him he heard the wide yells of the rustlers as they suddenly found them-

selves hemmed in by the converging groups of men, swinging around both sides of the herd. He slid the Colt from
its holster, lined it up on the head and shoulders of a man
who leapt out of the thick brush, tried to run for his horse.

The gun kicked against Lance's wrist and he saw the
man throw up his arms and then collapse on to his face in
the rough, stringy grass. He did not move as Lance rode
past him, swinging round to meet the gunfire that came
from the group of scattered boulders on the edge of the
spread where most of the rustlers were holed up. The
crash of another shot sounded in sharp, angry counter to
the deep-throated bellow of the steers.

An instant, and then there were more rustlers forming
up around the men in the rocks, this time men on horseback, who tried to loose off shots in Lance's direction,
hoping thereby to give their companions a chance to
reach their mounts and saddle up.

Swiftly, almost without pausing to think, Lance rode
down on them, cutting his mount through the boulders.
Others were riding with him. He could not make out their
faces in the rain-dripping darkness, but they were firing
incessantly now, the muzzle flashes of their guns glancing
redly through the blackness of the night. More shots came
in jagged, uneven rhythm from the rocks. A man close to
Lance swayed in his saddle, uttering a loud cry, clutching
at his smashed shoulder as he yelled. He tried to hang on
to the reins with his good hand, dropping the gun, then
pitched sideways, one foot caught in the stirrups, the
frightened mount dragging him over the rough ground.
Then his fingers loosened and he slipped out of the
saddle, to land in a crumpled heap several yards away.

Lance sent the sorrel racing forward now. His Colt
flared savagely in the night. Another man, lifting his head
from among the boulders, suddenly screamed and fell
back out of sight. He did not reappear.

Diego bored in, firing swiftly and savagely. More men
fell among the rocks. Those on horseback suddenly
wheeled their mounts, spurring them back towards the

hills on the horizon. They had evidently seen the danger, knew that if they hung around any longer they would be crowded away from their companions among the boulders and driven back on to the herd, and once they were among that mass of horn and muscle they would be finished, those needle-sharp horns ripping and tearing through flesh and bone.

Now, as far as the rustlers were concerned, they hadn't a chance. Once those men with Diego came riding round the other rim of the herd they must have known that they had lost. It was time for them to go.

Shots continued to follow them as they thundered off into the night. Then Lance turned his attention to the men still holed up in the rocks. For a moment there was silence as the guns stopped firing. Diego moved his mount forward a little way, sat tall and straight in the saddle and called harshly: 'All right, you *hombres*, are you coming out peaceful like, or do we have to come in and take you the hard way?'

A pause, then a voice called from the darkness: 'We ain't throwing out our guns, damn you! You'll have to come and take 'em.'

'If that's the way you want it.'

Lance had been listening to the voice from the shadows. He placed its source less than twenty yards from where he sat, a little to his right. But although he probed the blackness with his eyes, he could make out nothing of the man. No doubt he was crouched down behind the rocks, taking care not to expose himself to any fire from below. Carefully Lance slid from the saddle, edged forward. Out of the edge of his vision he noticed several of the other men doing likewise. No sense in trying to ride the rustlers down in those rocks. The only way to take them was on foot, maybe by working their way around to the rear of the men, coming up on them from behind, taking them by surprise, while a handful of men drew their fire from the front.

Crouching in the rocks he waited for a long moment,

searching the darkness. And as he waited there he remembered the way those men in Vengeance had treated him, making him marshal and then taking away his power to hold a killer in jail for fear of what Patten would do once he heard about it, regretting that they had offered him the job at all, hoping inwardly that he would resign, throwing in his badge. He turned cold and the anger and hatred came pouring through him once again, as it had so often in the past, changing him, chilling him to the bone, tightening every muscle and fibre of his being until his body seemed to be one huge and intolerable ache. He was sharply aware of the rain dripping from the brim of the wide hat, falling in front of his eyes. But the anger and patience made stone out of his body, and he knew that he could outwait any of the men near at hand. It was the waiting, he felt certain, that would eventually break these killers down.

Straining his ears, he caught the sudden long sigh that came from almost directly ahead of him. It was the sudden need for air that had betrayed the man, the intake of breath following the sigh which had given his position away. A second later he heard the sharp click as the man cocked his gun. Evidently he had realized he had given himself away and knew that any further sound would make no difference. Moments passed and then the men holed up in the rocks began to fire with pure recklessness, shooting with a wild abandon down the rocky slope. Their muzzle flashes were easily seen now and gunfire crashed and thundered in the night.

Lead flailed through the air close to Lance's head as he pulled himself down on the hard, wet rock, sucking air into his heaving lungs, taking careful aim before he pressed the trigger. There was no sense in wasting lead on these critters, he mused. If any of them were taken alive, he'd have to take them back to Vengeance and lock them up in the cells. And this time Benson would not be able to sign them loose in the morning. Rustling was still a hanging offence in this state and he had plenty of witnesses here.

There was a growing sense of excitement in him now. He had the feeling that he was really getting somewhere at that moment. He did not doubt for one moment that Patten had sent these men to rustle off some of Diego's herd and put the pressure on him to sell or get out.

SIX

PAY OFF AT VENGEANCE

The gunfight among the rocks on the edge of the Diego spread was short and savage. When it was over all but three of the rustlers trapped there had been killed. The others came out from their places of concealment, their hands held sullenly in the air, their faces tight, rain running into their eyes as they stood in front of Diego and Lance.

'I guess I ought to shoot the three of you down in cold blood,' rasped Diego harshly. He lifted the gun in his hand to cover the three men, his grin showing white in the shadow of his face as the three men backed away, one almost falling to his knees as he anticipated the smashing impact of a bullet.

'That wouldn't solve anything,' Lance told him sharply. 'We'll ride 'em back into Vengeance and lock them in the cells. They'll get a fair trial, but I reckon with the evidence you and your men can give against 'em there's only one verdict can come out of that trial and only one sentence.'

'Then why waste time getting them back into town?' snarled one of the other men. 'We've lost two men, shot down by these *hombres*. If it's a rope they'll get anyway, we can sure oblige 'em right now.'

Lance shook his head sharply and his right hand

hovered suggestively near the butt of his Colt. 'We do this thing my way, the legal way,' he said sharply. 'If you want law and order here, then you've got to start off the right way. Otherwise you'll never get it. Before you know where you are, you'll have rid yourselves of Patten only to have another man just as greedy and evil set himself up in his place and, in five years' time, or maybe before, you'll have to go through all of this again.'

There was a dull murmuring from the men crowding around the three prisoners, but once Diego holstered his gun, the others did likewise. Lance forced a quick breath down into his lungs. That had been a dangerous moment. He wondered what he would have done if they had not obeyed him. Even though the evidence was there that these man had been trying to rustle Diego's cattle, even though he had caught them red-handed, there were still the due processes of the law to go through before they were tried and sentenced.

A couple of the men rounded up three of the stray horses and they headed back in the direction of Vengeance. Lance rode a little to the rear of the tight bunch of men where he could keep an eye on them. After a while, Keene drifted back to him, rode alongside for several moments before speaking.

Then he said: 'You reckon that Benson will try to git these *hombres* free in the morning?'

'Very hard to say. I doubt it. If he does, then he'll find himself in trouble. It's one thing letting a wounded man out of jail, particularly when the only crime he's committed is trying to shoot down the marshal, and then trying to do the same thing for a bunch of rustlers caught in the act.'

'I hope you're right.' The other fell silent for a moment, then glanced sideways at the man who rode beside him. 'You thought of asking Benson about those deeds to the other ranches, Marshal?'

For a second Lance was caught off balance by the sudden shift of the other's question, then he shook his head. 'Maybe I'll get around to that some time,' he said softly. 'You figure there might be something in it?'

'Could be. He's a strange character, is Benson. Can't figure him out myself. I wish I knew what goes on in that lawyer's mind of his at times.'

'Now you ain't suggestin' that he's in cahoots with Patten, too?' inquired Lance incredulously.

'I ain't saying nothing,' growled the little man. He sat with one shoulder hunched higher than the other, lopsided in the saddle as if the wound was still paining him. 'But if I was you, I'd check a little further into our lawyer's background, where he was and what he was doing before he decided to drift into Vengeance.'

For a second Lance continued to look at the other, saw the old man's face as he stared straight ahead of him, looking neither to the right or left. He had the feeling that Keene knew more than he was saying – a lot more. But he also realized that even if he tried to press the other into talking, he would get nothing more out of him, at least not that particular night.

Vengeance lay silent in the darkness of early morning when they rode into town, pausing in front of the sheriff's office. Lance slid from the saddle, stood looking up at the three prisoners.

'All right, down on to your feet and then walk in ahead of me.' His tone brooked no argument and the men obeyed sullenly, Once they had been locked into the cells, he came back and stood on the boardwalk, looking up at the men in the saddle.

'You need any help with those polecats, Marshal?' asked Diego. His tone indicated that he hoped the other would answer in the affirmative, no doubt looking ahead to a possible escape attempt.

Lance shook his head. 'They'll be safe here until morning,' he said quietly. 'I don't reckon Patten will try to bust 'em out of jail before then.'

'Guess we could stick around in town until then,' said Keene laconically. 'No point in riding back to the ranch now. Soon be dawn anyways.'

They rode off along the silent street to the hotel, taking their mounts to the livery stable close by. Lance watched them for a moment, then went back inside the office, blew out the paraffin lamp, checked the prisoners, and went to sleep on the chair behind the desk, stretching out his long body in front of him. He was so beat after the night's work that he fell asleep almost instantly.

He woke to a loud knocking on the door, the sound dragging him up from the depths of exhausted sleep. Wearily he eased his body out of the chair, stretched and then moved to the door, opening it warily.

'Heard you'd got back to town, Marshal.' Benson stepped inside, took off his hat and laid it on top of the desk. He cast an appraising glance around the office, then looked in the direction of the cells.

'What's on your mind, Mister Benson?'

'Thought I'd come over and see if the talk that's been flying around town is true.'

'Depends on what it was you heard.'

The other forced a faint smile. 'They're saying that you rode out to meet some of the ranchers and that you brought back some prisoners with you.'

'Then you heard right,' Lance told him. He sat down at his desk again, rubbed the muscles at the back of his neck, kneading them with his long fingers. 'Diego and some of the ranchers were meeting at his place to discuss what they intended to do now that Patten seems hell bent on running them off the range piecemeal. While we were there some rustlers tried to make off with part of Diego's herd, and we rode hell for leather to head 'em off.'

'And did you?' There was a tightness in the lawyer's voice as he stared across at Lance, and a narrowness around the eyes which the other had not seen before.

'We got three in the cells,' said Lance casually. 'We left half a dozen lying dead in the rocks at the northern edge of the spread.'

Benson got to his feet.

'Have you any proof that they are Patten's men?'

'Nothing so far. But if any of those three were to talk, I guess we might find out something about 'em.' Grimly, he went on: 'It ain't likely that they'll keep their mouths shut just to let anybody else off scot free, not when they know they're going to hang anyhow.'

'You figuring on hanging them?' Surprise and something else tinged the lawyer's voice.

Lance sat up straight in the chair, met the other's gaze levelly. 'So far as I know, rustling is still a hanging offence in this state. They ain't got no defence against it. We caught 'em all red-handed.'

'I see. But do you think it's wise to hang them right away? After all, so long as they're held in jail they're quite safe and you might be able to get something out of them.'

Lance shrugged. 'Maybe there's something in what you say,' he agreed. There was something more behind the other's anxiety to make sure that there was no lynching party here in Vengeance. He wasn't merely thinking of the good name of the town either. Lance felt certain of that.

'Mind if I see the prisoners, Marshal?' Benson turned towards the passage leading back into the jail.

'Not at all. Guess it won't do any harm.' Lance led the way to the cells. 'Can't let you inside with any of 'em though, I'm afraid.'

'That'll be all right. Just want to see if I can get anything out of them that might help you.'

It was several seconds before Lance realized that this was one of the strangely jarring notes he had been waiting for ever since the other had walked into the office. He did not believe that the other could change his mind so quickly. But nevertheless, there was no point in showing his hand right now, just in case Keene had been right and there was some tie-up between Benson and Patten.

Half an hour later Lance walked over to the hotel for breakfast. He sat at his usual seat where he could see all that was happening in Vengeance. While he was still eating the ranchers who had accompanied him during the night came downstairs and joined him at the table. Diego said thinly: 'Any trouble from those prisoners of yours, Marshal?'

'None so far. Benson came along bright and early and asked to have a word with them. He left about five minutes ago, saw him making his way back to his office.'

'Benson!' Keene almost spat the other's name out, twisting his lips into a wry grin. 'You still trusting that lawyer, Marshal?'

'Got nothing against him at the moment,' Lance retaliated. 'Until I have, I got to treat him as I find him.'

'Wouldn't surprise me none if he ain't had a heart-to-heart talk with them critters and promised to get word through to Patten, if'n he don't already know about them being locked up here.'

'Now why should he do a thing like that?' interrupted one of the other men, staring at Keene over the rim of his coffee cup. 'Seems to be you're suspicious of everybody.'

'Got a right to be,' declared the other. 'My ranch was burned down about my ears by Patten's gunmen. I got a score to settle with him.'

Diego interrupted him, pointing through the window. 'Could be that you're right, Herb,' he said thickly. 'What do you make of that, Marshal?'

Lance turned his head quickly, following the direction of the other's pointing finger. Benson had ridden out of the narrow intersecting alley, sitting a mite uncomfortably in the saddle, as if unaccustomed to riding horseback. He edged his mount into the middle of the street, threw a swift glance up and down it, then rode out of town, heading in the direction of the Lazy K ranch.

'Now if he ain't going to warn Patten, I'll eat my hat,' declared the old man, nodding wisely.

It was high noon in Vengeance when the sound of a rider coming into town brought Lance Turner to the door of the office, stepping out quickly. There were ten other men with him as Diego reined his mount in front of the building and slid quickly from the saddle, booted heels hitting the ground before the horse had come to a halt.

'They're on their way,' he rasped harshly. 'Spotted 'em heading this way along the trail.'

'How far?' asked Lance quickly. 'And how fast?'

'Couple of miles, not more. And fast. They'll be here in ten minutes.'

Lance nodded decisively. 'Better get into position,' he said thinly. 'They may decide to back down when they see we mean business, but in case they don't we'll have to shoot it out with them.' He glanced back at Diego. 'Did you see Patten riding with that bunch?'

'Very likely he was, but I couldn't be sure. Too far away and I didn't stick around to let them get close enough. I just hightailed it right back here.'

Lance signalled to the waiting men, watched from the boardwalk as they made their way swiftly to both sides of the street. A narrow barricade had been set up along the street, built of wooden beams, it lay across the street from one side to the other. Not a formidable obstacle, Lance reflected, but one that was sufficient to make a man think twice about trying to crash through it. The tightness rose within him as he went back for a moment into the office, picked up the high-powered Winchester from the rack, checked it briefly. He was on the point of going out again when a shout from the direction of the cells halted him. 'You there, Marshal?'

'Sure, I'm here.'

'Sounded like some *hombre* in a hurry back there a minute ago,' called the rough voice. 'Could it have been one of your men riding in to warn you that Patten is on his way into Vengeance?'

'What if it was?'

'Reckon you'd do well to let us loose, Marshal. Patten ain't going to stop until we're busted out of this place and you know it. He'll tree this town and everything in it. Wait and see.'

'I'll wait,' said Lance evenly. 'I ain't aiming to go anywhere.'

Outside he glanced along the dusty street. There was a moment of utter silence which blended well with the heat haze that hung over everything, then he heard the slowly approaching rhythmic tread of horses' hooves from the far end of town. There, sitting their mounts with a deceptive ease, were Wayne Patten and perhaps thirty of his gunmen ranged at his back. One step after another they walked their mounts down the main street of Vengeance.

Just beyond the barrier, perhaps ten feet away, Patten lifted a hand. The men reined their mounts, sat waiting. There were no words, but each man held his hand poised above his gun.

For a long moment there was tension crackling along the street. It flowed like a breeze in the still air, deep and tangible. Then it was broken abruptly as Lance walked forward to the edge of the boardwalk and called: 'All right, Patten, that's far enough. If you've got anything to say, let's have it and then ride on out of Vengeance. We don't want any trouble here but if you're keen on making it, then by God, you shall have it.'

Patten turned his eyes on Lance, narrowed them to mere slits. He sat rock still in the saddle, running his gaze over the other. Then he glanced down at the barrier that stretched across the street, and a faintly derisive grin curled the thin lips.

'Are you figuring on stopping me yourself, Marshal, and with this barrier?' he asked tautly.

'I'm asking you a question, Patten,' Lance repeated himself. 'If you want to say anything, spill it.'

'All right.' The other lifted his hand away from his gun, supremely confident that he had everything in hand now. 'I understand that you have three of my men locked away in that jail of yours on some kind of charge or other. I want those men and I want them now. If you turn them loose to me, then we'll say no more about this – little misunderstanding.'

'Those men were caught trying to rustle cattle last night,' Lance said thinly. 'I brought them in myself.

They'll stay here until a trial is fixed, and after that, since the evidence is overwhelming against them, they'll hang. That's the penalty for rustling in this state.'

Patten's hand clenched and unclenched on the reins and his face purpled a little with barely controlled fury. But his tone was even and steady as he said: 'Reckon you didn't hear me right, Marshal. I want those men of mine and I'm not leaving town without them. You'll save yourself a lot of trouble if you would just open up the cells and hand them over. If you don't, then my patience will soon be exhausted and I'll have my men take this town apart.'

His eyes were bright with challenge now, his head thrust forward a little on the bull-like neck.

'Somehow, I don't think you or your men are going to do anything.' Lance stepped back a couple of paces. 'Better take a look around you before you decide to go for your guns. There are a dozen rifles lined up on you. Maybe we won't get everyone of you with the first shot but, by God, Patten, you'll be the first to die and most of your men will go with you, before you have a chance to reach for your guns.'

He saw the other turn his head sharply, his gaze flicking from one side of the street to the other, saw the look of angry surprise, of baffled fury on his face as he realized that he had ridden into a trap. The barrels of the rifles, lined up on the tightly bunched men from the Lazy K, projected from the windows of the buildings nearby on either side of the main street, or from behind the large water barrels on the edge of the boardwalks.

'Now just turn around and ride out of town,' Lance advised gently, but with a note of menace in his voice. 'Keep on riding, too, if you know what's good for you.'

For a second the other regarded him with lips thinned back across his teeth, and the thought lived in his mind that he might have a chance to go for his weapon and gun down Lance before any of the waiting men could loose off a killing shot. Then the thought left him, sanity prevailed, and he suddenly wheeled his mount, thrusting back against the men directly behind him. They all turned and began to pace back along the street.

Lance eased his breath from between tightened lips. He had not expected Patten to back down as quickly as that. There was something wrong here. A moment later he knew what it was. Patten must have been speaking to his men in an undertone as they rode away. Thirty yards along the road and they suddenly uttered loud, shrill cries, scattering their mounts in all directions, slipping from the saddles and throwing themselves down on to the ground, rolling for the boardwalks. Instinctively Lance brought up the rifle and loosed off a couple of shots, saw the dirt spurt up around the rolling body of one of the men, but he knew that neither of the shots had gone home.

From both sides Diego and the other ranchers opened fire, sending shots bucketing along the street. A man yelled with the agony of a shattered shoulder, suddenly got to his feet and tried to run back, staggering blindly from one side to the other.

He had gone less than half a dozen paces before a rifle cracked on the opposite side of the street and the man went down and lay still. A window broke into a hundred shards of glittering glass over Lance's head. Another shot tore long wooden splinters from the post of the veranda. He could feel the sweat beading his forehead now and running in narrow streams along his lean jaws. He continued to fire with the Winchester until he had spent his last shell, then laid it on one side and used the Colt, balancing it carefully and easily in his hand.

Deep in the thundering rush of feeling that overwhelmed him, the chill of some strange and darkly mysterious thought came in countercurrent. He guessed now that Benson had been the man who had ridden out to warn the other of the men held in the jail. Just why had the lawyer done that? What was the connection between him and Patten? Did one have some strange kind of hold over the other? It was possible, but he would never have believed it had he not seen Benson riding out less than two hours before Patten had ridden into Vengeance seeking those men. There might, of course, be some other explanation, but at the moment he could think of none.

Two slugs hummed viciously close to his head and he threw himself on one side, hitting the wooden slats of the boardwalk with a stunning force that sent a blast of agony through the muscles of his left arm. He bit down on the grunt of pain, tried to see where those shots had come from. It was a grim and cold business, shooting down these men who threatened law and order in this town. No quarter was asked and none given. No mercy.

Dimly he heard Patten's loud voice yelling orders, caught a fragmentary glimpse of him a moment later, hugging the dark shadows on the far side of the street. Swiftly he snapped a shot at the man, but Patten had dropped behind the handrail and the shot went wide.

The firing burst up again with a sultry violence, blending strangely with the heat that pressed down from the bright, clear blue of the sky. Three more of Patten's men died. They were still at a disadvantage even though they still outnumbered the ranchers. The defensive position had been planned during the long hours of the morning, ever since it had been obvious that Patten would come riding in with his men.

Two men came rushing from the direction of the saloon, ten yards beyond the barrier. For a moment they paused in the middle of the street, their guns out, blazing savagely along both sides of the street, their slugs cutting through the wooden uprights. Lance edged forward until he reached the end of the boardwalk, where he could see the two men clearly. Easing his long body out flat on the wooden slats, he loosed off a couple of shots, saw one man stagger, then throw up his arms and drop back. He was dead before he hit the ground. The other man swung his guns to cover Lance, fired two shots that went wild, then stumbled forward as a couple of bullets took him full in the chest. There was a look of stark, stupefied amazement on his face as the muscles slackened. His guns gave twin

bursts of flame as he fell forward, bullets chewing into the
dirt in front of him. Lance sucked in a deep breath and
steadied himself. It was impossible to see where Patten had
hidden himself, but he could vaguely hear the other still
yelling orders to his men.

Out of the corner of his eye he glimpsed one of the
ranchers suddenly fall forward as if all of the starch had
gone out of his body. He fell without a sound, arms
outflung, the gun dropping into the street from his dead
fingers. Gripping the Colt hard, Lance slitted his eyes
against the harsh glare of the sun, tried to estimate where
that shot had come from. Smoke eddied and whirled
about him now and he could feel the crush of Patten's
men not so very far away, moving forward slowly, the crash
of their guns loud in his ears, a thunderous, deafening
sound. The hurried thumping of his heart kept uneven
rhythm with the harsh breathing of old Herb Keene, lying
only a few feet away, eyes bright and staring as he tried to
glimpse a target without exposing himself to the intense
return fire.

The orange flame from the rifle was just visible a
second later and the bullet tore into the wood less than an
inch from his body, ricocheting off into the distance with
the muted whine of tortured metal. Lance pressed himself
hard against the unyielding surface of the wood, knowing
instinctively that a second slug was on its way. It hummed
through the air scant inches above his head and ploughed
into the wooden wall of the building behind him. But he
knew now where that gunman was. Not in the street with
the other killers. Somehow he had managed to get into
the saloon and move into one of the upper rooms. He was
now crouched behind the window of one of the rooms,
lifting his head only long enough to take aim and squeeze
the trigger of the Winchester.

When he started to move again, Lance edged forward
with his shoulders hunched, knees bent slightly under his
body, the Colt held tightly in the palm of his hand, one eye
on the window where the gunman was hidden. The

hammer of the Colt was held at full cock. Slowly he shifted his weight from one foot to the other, steadied himself for an instant, then flung his body forward across the narrow space that divided the boardwalk from the other side of the alley. Desperately, knowing that a bullet might be following him, he flung himself forward the last couple of feet, crashed behind the rail and swung himself round on to his side in the same instant, bringing the Colt up in his right hand. There was a sudden movement at the window where he had pinpointed the killer. The other had been expecting some move from him, but that sudden dash had obviously taken him by surprise for his body was just visible as he tried to bring the rifle to bear. Sighting swift and sure, Lance let go the hammer, felt the Colt kick back in his hand, saw the gunslick lurch as the slug took him in the chest, pitching him forward. For a second he hung over the ledge of the window, then slid forward, his body hurtling down to crash with a sickening thud on the boardwalk below.

Very carefully Lance eased himself upright. From somewhere in the shadows of the far side of the street he could hear Patten yelling to his men and a few moments later, guns still blazing, they piled out from their hiding places, ran for the waiting horses, clambered into the saddle and rode swiftly out of town, a handful of shots whistling along the street after them.

'Let 'em go,' Lance yelled harshly. He stood up and moved out into the street, still cautious, although he doubted if this was a trap. Patten wasn't likely to have left any of his men still around simply in the hope of killing him without warning.

He holstered his gun. Around him, Herb Keene, Diego and the others rose to their feet and moved forward, staring down at the bodies of the men who had been killed. At the edge of town, at the far end of the street, the dust still hung in the air, dust thrown up by the hooves of the riders' mounts as they had ridden swiftly out of town.

'Reckon they'll be back, Marshal?' grunted Diego. He

thrust the gun back into its holster with a final gesture, mouth set in a grim, tight line.

'Hard to say. He'll come back some time, but as to when I'm not sure. He's taken a beating that he didn't expect and that'll mean he'll be doubly dangerous the next time he tries anything. He knows that, in the eyes of his men, he'll have to finish us off the next time. Because after that, if he loses, he'll never get another chance. His leadership will count for nothing as far as those hired killers are concerned. They'll only follow a man if he can destroy all opposition. At the moment Patten must be feeling like a fool.'

Diego rubbed his stubbled chin. He glanced up at the sun, high in the heavens, screwing up his eyes. 'I'd like to be able to stick around in town, just in case he does come back, Marshal, but, like the rest of the men here, we've got work to do on our own spreads. And what happened to my cattle could happen to anybody.'

'I reckon you're right.' Lance nodded. 'Thanks for your help here, anyway. I doubt if he'll come back today.' He glanced round at one of the other men. 'Do you reckon you could bring that dynamite into town today? If I could have some of that, I reckon I might be able to hold 'em off, or at least even the odds a little.'

'Sure thing, Marshal,' nodded the other. 'I'll bring it in myself this evenin'.'

True to his word, the other returned shortly before nightfall, a couple of war bags slung across the front of his saddle. Coming into the sheriff's office, he placed them carefully on top of the desk, glancing across at Lance. 'There you are, Marshal. What you mean to do with this stuff, I don't aim to know. But whatever it is, better handle it carefully. It's powerful stuff and one little mistake is all you need.'

Lance gave a quick nod. 'I'll be careful,' he promised. 'Did you see any sign of Patten or his men on your way here?'

'Saw a handful of riders off to the south, but too far away to say who they were. They seemed to be heading away from Vengeance, so I guess they weren't any of Patten's men.'

'Could be a bluff on his part,' mused Lance. 'Or maybe he's sending them around so they can come in from the other direction and take us from the rear.'

'Could be,' agreed the other. He stirred restlessly. 'Reckon I'd better be riding back, Marshal. Don't like leaving the ranch after dark. Patten may decide to try for it, instead of hitting the town as we figure.'

'Sure.' Lance got to his feet, moved to the door with the other. Already the sky in the east was beginning to purple and the hills on the horizon were almost lost against the background of the coming night. The sun hung poised on the western skyline, ready to drop out of sight at a moment's notice. Lance watched as the other saddled up, then wheeled his mount and rode swiftly out of town.

There was a strangely empty sense of loneliness in him as he stood there, staring out along the deserted street. After the gun battle that morning, the people of Vengeance seemed to have gone indoors, to have withdrawn into the comparative safety of the houses and stores, knowing by some strange instinct that sudden death and flaring guns could begin again without any warning, that the showdown was now inevitable and soon gun thunder would roar and echo again in the street of Vengeance.

Unconsciously, Lance looked towards the far horizons, and it was almost as if he could see beyond the undulating skyline and see the bunch of riders saddling up on the Lazy K ranch, riders led by a tight-lipped man, determined that this time nothing was going to go wrong, that he would ride into Vengeance and gun down the man who stood in his way. Patten was there. And no matter how many hours or days passed, Patten was coming with vengeance in his heart.

Was it possible for him to stand alone against these

men, this army of hired killers? Had the fact that he had
defeated them once in the town, with the help of a small
number of men, been sufficient to show the townsfolk that
Patten could be stopped and destroyed if only they would
back him to the hilt? Somehow he doubted it, but he
needed some form of help if he was to defeat this man and
bring law and order to Vengeance.

Slowly he made his way along the street, a solitary man,
walking alone in the rapidly lengthening shadows, feet
whispering quietly in the dust. There were some lights
showing yellowly through the windows on either side of
the street, and from the direction of the saloon he heard
the tinny, tinkling notes of the piano and an occasional
harsh roar of laughter.

Crossing the street, he pushed open the doors of the
saloon and walked inside. For a moment he stood there,
his eyes flicking over the men at the tables or ranged along
the bar, at the white-aproned barkeeper standing with his
weight resting on his elbows. A sudden uneasy silence fell
over the room. Wherever he glanced, he saw the men look
away from him, unable to meet his gaze, as if they had
guessed why he was there and wanted him to ignore them
completely. Most of them, he saw, wore guns and he knew
that they could use them. But would they if he tried to
deputise them into a posse, to go out and face Patten?

Slowly he walked over to the bar, aware that every eye in
the room was following him.

'Rye,' he said quietly.

The barkeep poured the drink, stood for a moment
with the bottle still in his hand, holding it poised over the
bar. Then he placed it down close to Lance's hand. 'You
expecting trouble, Marshal?' he asked harshly.

'Could be. It seems the right kind of night for it.' Lance
did not look up but stared at the amber liquid in his glass,
swirling it around gently in his hands. 'What are you figuring on doing if Patten does come riding into town tonight
with some of his men, ready to take the place apart? They
won't stop at the sheriff's office, you know. They'll wreck

the saloon, the hotel and most of the stores. Or haven't you bothered to think about that?'

The other wet his thick lips, stared at Lance out of puffy eyes. He pulled a wet cloth from his apron pocket and began to wipe the stains from the top of the bar with industrious movement of his arm.

'I don't see that Patten has got anything against me, Marshal. I'm neutral as far as this feud is concerned. Don't see any real reason why he should break up the saloon.'

'No?' Lance lifted his brows a little. He made a half-turn from the bar, surveyed the other men in the saloon. Raising his voice a little so that every man there could hear him, he said harshly: 'Do you all reckon that this is just a matter between Patten and me? If you do, then you're bigger fools than I figured. It's no longer as simple as that. He's trying to drive the other ranchers out of the territory so that he can step in and take over. Then he'll be running this town, and if you don't jump whenever he tells you to, it'll be the last thing you'll do, because you won't have any law and order here to protect you.'

He paused. Nobody seemed to want to say anything. He let the silence grow for a while, then went on scathingly: 'You wanted me elected as marshal here. You gave me a badge and swore me in. Trouble was that you forgot to tell me that every man here was so yellowlivered I'd get no help when it came to a showdown.'

'Now steady on there, Marshal,' said one of the men hesitantly. Suspicion lay heavy in the saloon. 'We ain't gunmen. You can see that. Not like those professional killers Patten has got following him. What kind of a chance do you reckon we would stand against 'em?'

'We made a pretty good stand this noon,' Lance told them sharply, switching his gaze to some of the others. 'We showed Patten that he could be stopped and he outnumbered us, too.'

'Mebbe so,' grunted the other thinly, 'but the next time he comes he'll bring every man he has with him. He won't make the same mistake again.'

Lance stirred restlessly. 'Do I get any man to go with me when he does come? I'm asking for deputies now.'

They looked away again, staring at the ground or at each other, not wanting to meet his direct gaze. Lance turned to the barkeep, but the other shook his head heavily. 'I ain't going to face up to Patten and them gunslingers just for this.'

Lance set his lips into a tight line. 'I figure that you all deserve everything you get in this goddamed town.' His words lashed at them, biting through the silence. 'Patten isn't to blame for this situation, you all are – every man here. If you'd only decided to stand up for what you believed in, what you thought was right, Patten would never have become the menace he is today. You could have ridden out there and destroyed him utterly, made it impossible for anybody else to set himself up like that. But instead, you just sat back and let things go their own way, so long as you didn't have to fight for what you thought was right, so long as there was somebody else fool enough to do the fighting for you. Pardee was sheriff when I first came into Vengeance. A good man, a straight man. But when the showdown with Patten came, did anybody stand with him and fight?

'No. You all deserted him. You're as much responsible for his death as Patten is and the man who actually pulled the trigger. Then you got Sloan and you really deserved him. He was the sort of man you ought to have here. Somebody who cares nothing for you or for the law. Then Patten could just ride into town and take it over.'

'We figure that if Patten rides into town and there's no opposition, maybe he'll behave peaceable,' broke in the bartender.

'Meaning that you want me to throw in my badge and pull out?' snapped Lance harshly, whirling on the other.

The bartender shrugged non-committally. 'It might be best for all concerned,' he murmured softly. 'After all, there are women and children in town who might get hurt if Patten rides in and shoots up the place.'

'And what sort of life do you figure these women and children will have to lead if he does take over as he threatens?'

There was no answer to that. The silence grew as Lance stared down at them, feeling the anger and the sense of disgust rising in him, threatening to swamp every other feeling in his brain. His hand reached down, fingers touching the cold steep of the Colt. 'Well, I don't intend to give in to Patten or to you.' His words fell into the muffling silence. 'I'm going to meet Patten if I have to do it alone.'

'You're a fool, Marshal,' said the man who had spoken first. 'You'll only end up as Pardee did – a candidate for Boot Hill.'

'Mebbe so. But you can be sure that I'll take Patten with me, even if it's only to avenge Pardee's death.'

'*So it was Patten who ordered my father's death.*' The words were a ringing harshness and Lance turned quickly to face the door. Grace Pardee stood just inside, staring across at him, and in the glow from the lamps her face had a shadowed, tight expression, her eyes bright and angry. By her sides the small hands were clenched into tight fists and she seemed to be holding herself in only with a tremendous physical effort. She stepped further into the saloon and stared round at the men at the tables.

'You all knew my father,' she said, bitterness edging her voice. 'You knew that he was a good man, that he always did everything as he saw it. To him, this town and everybody in it meant everything. And, because of that, he was shot down in cold blood, shot down in the street because he wanted to protect you all. And now, when a man comes along who'll do the same for you as my father tried to do, you still refuse to back him up. What kind of men are you?' Her voice was a ringing, angry sound in the hushed room.

The men stirred uncomfortably at the tables. If they had been unwilling to meet Lance's glance, they were even more so to meet the girl's fiery stare. Her lips curled into a distasteful expression.

'I thought so. Cowards! All of you! There isn't a single man among you.' Her voice almost broke at that point but, with an effort, she went on: 'I think I know now that my father died in vain. Not a single one of you is worth saving. There isn't a man here who's worth fighting or dying for.'

'Now don't take on so, Miss Pardee,' interrupted one of the men near the back of the room. 'You don't know what this *hombre* Patten is like, or the men who ride with him. Ain't no point in everyone here getting killed. I'm willing to take my chance with the next man, but there ain't no chance with them.'

Grace Pardee whirled on him, then her shoulders sagged a little as she stood there, shaking her head a little. 'I've said my piece,' she said softly, and it was as if all of the fight had suddenly gone from her, leaving her weak and defenceless. For a moment she stood silent, then turned and stumbled out of the saloon, into the night, the doors whispering shut behind her. In three quick strides Lance had gone out into the street behind her, but she was nowhere in sight. He hesitated for a moment, then turned towards the office. At the moment he had more important work to do.

SEVEN

A TRAP IS SET

It was fully dark when Lance swung up into the saddle, sat for a long moment listening to the faint noises of the night, then leaned forward and checked the war bags tied securely to the pommel of the saddle. He felt a little nervous at the thought of all that explosive within a few inches of his body, but soon forced the thought away. There was danger in this, of course. He did not know for sure which way Patten and his men would come, whether they would split into two groups and move into town from both ends of the trail. If they did that, then there was little he could do about it. He could only destroy one bunch moving along the trail from the north. He guessed that was the way they would come.

Patten was a man who had his pride. He would want everyone in Vengeance to know when he came riding in and he would do it openly, if only to show that he held the whip hand, that this upstart marshal had no chance at all against him. Lance was relying on this when he had formulated his plan of action. Everything depended on him being able to put as many of Patten's men out of action at once as possible.

Gigging the sorrel forward, he paced the street, then headed north along the trail in the direction of the Lazy K spread. He doubted if he would bump into any of Patten's

123

trail crew on the way, unless they were moving into Vengeance sooner than he had figured. Once outside the town, he strained his ears to identify the tiny sounds that were all around him, seeking to separate the faint rustle of the wind in the dry branches of the mesquite from the lingering, half-lost echoes that might come of men travelling hard and fast in the distance.

For a while, as he rode, he put most of his attention on speculation as to why Benson had thrown in his lot with Patten and found it baffling. Was it merely because the lawyer, with a keen eye to the future and his own position in Vengeance, had decided that, with only the one man standing against Patten, the outcome of this battle was assured and he wanted to throw in his hand on the winning side? Or was there something deeper to it than that? Surely the other must have known that he would be seen, heading out of town in the direction of Patten's spread, and the fact that within two hours Patten had showed up in town, looking for the release of his men, would surely be looked upon as something more than mere coincidence.

The more he thought about it, the more baffling it became and, after a while, he turned his thoughts to the sodbusters on the outskirts of town, wondering if they would fight when the showdown came, whether they would back him against Patten. They might fight, but with them one could never be sure. They were the pioneers of this new country now, moving in droves westward, breaking in new ground, building their settlements near the towns, and he had the feeling that if it did come to a showdown, then they would fight if only to protect their homesteads and families from men like Patten. Most of the sodbusters were men who had been through the war, had been tempered by it and who knew that if you really wanted anything bad enough, then you had to fight for it, that very often there was no other way. Now they had their families and their homes to fight for and not just the abstract ideals for which they had been asked to fight in the war.

Half a mile further on he entered thick, rough timber, and the hollow echoes of his horse's hooves on the hard earth seemed to be reflected back from the trees that reared up on either side of him. He could just make out the stars through breaks in the overhead canopy of branches and leaves, and was glad when he rode out into the open again. He judged that he was a little more than a mile or so out of town, and began to look about him for a suitable place to lay his trap. Cool wind sifted down from the hills in the near distance and, five minutes later, pushing his vision ahead of him through the darkness, he made out the place he was looking for where a narrow, winding creek ran across the trail and the ground sloped down to it from either direction. There were plenty of rocks here, too, which suited his purpose admirably.

Dismounting, he lifted down the war bags and placed them on one of the large, flat-topped boulders at the edge of the trail. Around him he could hear nothing but the faint ripple of the water over the stony bed of the creek. There was a sense of urgency in him now that gave him no rest.

In the dimness he located two hollows on either side of the trail among the rocks, hollows that were partially filled with earth, where the rain had washed the soil down from above, filling the cracks among the rocks. Very carefully, taking his time, he laid the charges of explosive, pushing the fuses home. When he had finished, he glanced about him, satisfied. There were still so many things here that could go wrong, he told himself fiercely. He only knew the burning speed of that fuse approximately. If Patten hurried his men more than usual, or took his time once they were lit, then the charges could conceivably go off before they were there or after they had passed this spot. He was relying on them having to slow their pace to ford the stream here, and that ought to give him the slight pause that he needed. If they rode over, tightly bunched together, so much the better. The explosive was buried among the boulders on either side of the trail, but not so deeply buried there that they would muffle the blast. Any man riding the trail at that point when the charges blew was as good as dead.

As he rode back into Vengeance, Lance could feel the tension in his body beginning to mount. There were so many imponderables that it was impossible for anyone to formulate a plan which had more than a fifty-fifty chance of success. He knew that there was just the chance that Patten would get his men together and ride into Vengeance that night, before dawn, unable to contain his anger at the defeat he had suffered at Lance's hands. He had been used to the ways of violence in the past, but now everything seemed to be cloaked in uncertainties and difficulties.

The town slept as he rode in from the north, pacing his mount slowly along the shadowed street. Moonlight threw long streaks of blackness among the squat buildings and he felt the loneliness grow in him as his eyes took in the silent houses, the saloon, now shuttered and barred, the last of the drunks gone, leaving the place deserted until the next night. But what of the night after that, Lance thought bitterly. And all of the other nights and days which were to come. Where would Vengeance be then? Run by Patten and the crooked lawmen he would put into office, once they had buried Lance Turner up there in the cemetery on the hill overlooking the town.

Unlocking the door of the office, he went inside, stretching himself out loosely in the chair behind the desk for the second time, after checking that the three prisoners he had brought in the previous night were still there. Sleep was a long time in coming that night, even though his body was dead beat, a dull ache suffusing through every limb. He could not help thinking of those two charges of explosive packed out there in the rocks, waiting only to be touched with the end of a cigarette for the fuses to burn throughout their snaking length, and then the twin explosions, shattering rock, blowing the boulders to dust and flying chips that would do as much harm to a man nearby as a bullet, ripping his body to shreds.

For what seemed an eternity he sat there, listening to the utter silence outside, turning things over in his mind in an attempt to find an answer to some of the urgent problems that faced him, but unable to do so. Then, finally, he fell into an uneasy doze, from which he woke to find the pale light of an early dawn slanting through the windows, highlighting every object in the room. Getting slowly to his feet, stretching his long body to ease the bruises in each limb, he made his way back to the cells, rattled on the bars with the barrel of the gun. The men inside stirred sullenly, then got to their feet.

'Just figured you might like to know that Patten is probably going to try to bust up the town today,' he said easily, stopping any of the signs of strain from showing through on his face. 'He may think he can pull you out of jail. If he does, then he's wrong.'

'What makes you think that, Marshal?' sneered one of the men harshly. 'You still reckon that you can stand up to Patten when he comes riding in? Why don't you take a look at things as they really are, Turner. You don't stand for anything in this town any longer. They don't want you here any more than Patten does. They know you're only a menace now. You're not the big man that you think you are.'

'Mebbe not, but I'll tell you all this.' Lance gritted the words out slowly and distinctly, forming them with a savage emphasis. 'I'm still the law here and so far there ain't a thing that the townsfolk can do about it. I signed that contract as marshal, and if they're now regrettin' it, then it's just too bad for all concerned. But I'll see each one of you three shot before I let Patten take you outa here and turn you loose to start more plunderin' and rustlin'.'

That silenced them. After he'd put food and water into each cell, checked the locks, he went into the office, made himself some hot coffee on the stove and fried a plate of bacon and potatoes. Once he had eaten he felt a little better. There was still a deep tiredness in him, and the feel-

ing that today was going to see the end of something as far
as he was concerned. If only he could foresee what Patten
intended to do, he would have felt a lot easier in his mind.
As it was, there were so many things with his hastily formulated plan that could go wrong that he did not pause to
consider the odds against success. All he did know was that
if he failed, then the town was wide open for Patten and
his gunslicks to ride in and take over, and it might be many
years before proper law and order was re-established here.
But, of course, it would not concern him. By that time he
would be dead and no doubt forgotten by most of the folk
there.

For a second his mind dwelt on Grace Pardeen, turning
over an image in his mind. There could be a softness
about her that any man would have desired, he thought,
even though he himself had seen only the hard exterior
brought on by the thought of revenge for the slaying of
her father. What would she do if Patten succeeded in
getting rid of him and riding into town? Live with the
knowledge that it had been Patten who had ordered her
father's death – or would she try to kill him herself? Either
way, life for her was not going to be very pleasant.

He finished his coffee, buckled on the heavy gunbelt,
checked that each loop was filled with a bullet, then
stepped outside, drawing air deeply into his lungs.
Vengeance was just beginning to stir, but there was still an
air of sleepy quietness about the town. Several yards away
he saw one of the men move into the livery stable and
there was another sweeping the steps of the hotel with a
hickory broom.

The sun was not yet up and the town still lay in shadow
although the crests of the tall hills in the distance were
tinged with red and there was a faint heat in the air, a
hazing stillness that promised another hot day. He whistled up his mount, knew that several pairs of eyes were
watching him as he swung up into the saddle, wondering
what he intended to do. For a second there was a harsh
stirring of anger deep within him. Damn them all, he

thought savagely, damn the whole town for its attitude towards him now that he had done as they had asked and taken on this job of marshal. Never in his whole career had he met up with so thankless a task. It would serve every one of them right if he suddenly threw in the badge and quit, rode out of town with the gold he had panned and hewn from the rocks, and kept on riding south and east, until he was as far away from this god-forsaken town as possible, where no one had even heard of Vengeance. But the thought that this was probably what they really wanted him to do, coupled with the pride in him and his harsh hatred of Patten and all that he stood for, told him that he would never quit now.

In the dim, grey light of the early morning he rode along the street of Vengeance, out along the winding trail to the north. Soon, he knew, Patten would come riding in. Already he had probably gathered his gunhawks together. He lit a smoke and drew it deeply and luxuriously into his lungs as he rode, eyes shifting from one side to the other, missing nothing, for out here, he knew, death could strike from many directions with the speed of a rattler, and a man was either fast with a gun – or dead.

Half an hour later he came in sight of the wooded stretch of ground. Beyond it lay the narrow creek. And on either side of the trail at that point, tucked away in the folds of ground among the rocks, were the two charges of explosive with the fuses already in place, snaking over the boulders. It would be the work of a single moment to light them both with one of the sulphur matches in his pocket, but he would have to estimate the length of time it would take them to burn through, time to give himself a chance to get far enough away not to be caught in the open by the blast, yet near enough to be able to open fire on any men still left alive. And on top of this, he had to judge things closely so that Patten and his gunslicks were close enough to the charges when they went off to catch the full blast of them.

He came out of the timber, reined his mount at the

edge of the trail, keeping back under cover where he could look down and watch the trail for several miles, running almost due north from his vantage point. The prairie lay spread out in front of him, a mass of greens and browns in the light of the rising sun. As yet there was no sign of life, no movement out there and, although he strained his ears, he could not pick out the sound of riders approaching which would be the first indication he had of trouble heading in his direction.

He settled down to wait. From where he sat it would be possible to pick out the Lazy K bunch while they were still the best part of three miles away. Even if they were riding hell for leather, that ought to still give him plenty of time to light those fuses and get under cover.

The sun lifted clear of the eastern horizon and the prairie began to shimmer in the growing heat head. Lance felt the sweat start out on his brow and wiped it away with the red handkerchief. The creek shone brilliantly in the sunlight some thirty yards away, flowing across the trail. A handful of stunted trees and thorn grew down to the bank and, at that point, where the trail narrowed, it would be possible for less than three men to ride side by side, and he guessed that here, if anywhere, they were bound to be tightly bunched.

He ran a dry tongue over dry lips, then reached for the canteen and drank slowly, swilling the cool liquid around his mouth before swallowing it. He had barely fastened it back on to the side of the saddle when his sharp gaze noticed the faint cloud of dust in the distance. As yet it was little more than a vague blur on the skyline, but his pulse quickened as he realized what it was. The dust thrown up by the hooves of horses ridden hard, heading towards him along the trail. The sight sent a little thrill racing through him, and his hand tightened on the reins in front of him. Slitting his eyes against the glare of the sun, now quite high in the cloudless heavens, he judged them to be the best part of five miles away, cutting across the prairie on to the broad trail out there to the north.

His stomach muscles tightened involuntarily, and he could feel the nerves in his arms and legs beginning to jump uncontrollably. Gigging his mount, he rode it slowly down the trail until he reached the short stretch of rocky ground that bordered the creek, when he slipped from the saddle and moved forward. The thunder of the approaching riders was loud in his ears now, and he waited for another minute, then struck a match and lit the nearer piece of fuse. It began to burn instantly, throwing off a faint haze of smoke. Moving quickly, he went over the trail and lit the other, made certain they were both burning satisfactorily, then went back to the sorrel and climbed up into the saddle. He could just make out the haze of smoke from the burning fuses, but by the time that bunch of riders arrived on the scene, they would have burned up into the rocks close to the explosive, and he reckoned none of the men with Patten would spot them. Even if they did, it would be too late for them to do anything. Once that fuse was lit and the powder train burning, it would be a very foolhardy man who would try to stop it.

Two minutes later he was back in the trees, nearly a hundred yards from the creek. He could see the riders clearly now, hunched low over their mounts, and judged there to be almost forty men with Patten, pushing their horses at a punishing pace. He let his breath escape from his lungs in a long-drawn sigh, eased the Colt in its holster. The tightness in him reached its peak. By now he could even make out Patten, riding furiously, raking spurs across his horse's flanks. Another thirty seconds and they would swing around the sharply angled curve in the trail, moving towards the creek.

He knew that so far he had not been seen, that Patten had no suspicions that anything was wrong. The men continued to come forward without altering their pace until they reached the bend. Then, jostling forward, they slowed their mounts slightly, putting them into the water. Lance held his breath until it began to hurt in his lungs. At any moment now, if he had judged things right, that explosive ought to blow, shattering the rocks and hurling them at the men from either side of the narrow trail.

Patten, he saw, was now at the rear of the bunch, pausing and urging his men across the creek. The first group put their mounts across, their progress slowed inevitably by the water and the slippery, treacherous stones on the bed of the creek.

The others came up behind them, thrusting and jostling. There was, as Lance had anticipated, a general melee in the middle of the creek. Then the first men had gained the nearer bank and were urging their horses up the steep sides. Still no sign that the explosive would blow at the right moment. A riot of thoughts raced through his mind as he sat tight and taut in the saddle among the trees, debating whether to open fire on them in an attempt to slow them up, knowing that if he had made any mistake in the timing of that fuse, it could mean the explosive would not go before the bunch had ridden on and, by that time, they would be between the explosive charges and himself.

Swiftly, acting on instinct, he pulled the Colt from its holster, aimed it at the leading man and squeezed the trigger. In the yelling and shouting from the men crossing the creek, the sharp crack of the gunshot passed almost unnoticed. But in that same instant the rider suddenly threw up his arms, lurched back in the saddle, a look of utter amazement on his grim features, then slipped sideways to fall under the pounding hooves of the horse behind him.

Sucking air sharply into his lungs, he aimed again, squeezing on the trigger, and dimly heard Patten's bulllike roar, saw the other on the far edge of the creek, staring across the water towards the trees, pointing with his left hand, while his right streaked for the gun in his belt. Then everything was lost, drowned utterly by the tremendous roar as the first charge went off, to be followed a split second later by the other. The bunch of riders was obliterated by the dust and fumes that rose from the rocks. For a moment Lance glimpsed the orange flash of flame from the twin explosions. Then the blast reached him and almost knocked him from the saddle.

Grimly he hung on, quietening the bucking sorrel as it reared nervously with a shrill whinney of fear at the sudden sound. Slowly the rumbling, reverberating echoes died away, reflected back by the hills in the distance as solid, individual thunderclaps. Along the trail the smoke and dust cleared only slowly in the still, heat-hazed air, clouding the rocks near the stream.

Vaguely Lance was able to make out the struggling, plunging shapes of the horses, thrown into utter confusion by the blast, and their shrill, frightened neighing rasped on his ears. Several of the men had been hurled from their saddles and lay unmoving on the ground among the scattered rocks and boulders, dead or unconscious.

A handful of men, wounded but still on their feet, were lunging for the shelter of the rocks, crouching down among them, unsure as to whether there would be any further explosions. They seemed bewildered by the titanic force of the twin detonations.

Lance snapped a couple of quickly aimed shots into them. A ragged volley came at him as other men, still in the saddle, men who had been still on the far edge of the creek when the blast had come, opened up on him. A rifle cracked from the bushes and Lance saw that Patten had escaped, apparently unhurt, his luck holding out to the last.

The bullet cut through the air close to Lance's head, tore through the trees at his back with a shrill flicker of sound. He jerked instinctively in the saddle, threw a couple of shots at the fleeting shapes as more men moved up to help Patten. The rancher ran forward a couple of yards, then dropped down out of sight behind the upthrusting boulders. Lance's reflex action had undoubtedly saved his life. Most of the men with Patten were still confused by the shots which poured into them, trying to pacify their mounts as they milled around endlessly in the shallow water of the creek. One reared up sharply, unseating the rider on its back, and the man toppled backward into the stream with a wild yell, splashing into the water, where he lay still, either dead or unconscious as his head hit the hard stones just below the surface.

But Patten had clearly sized up the situation instantly, could guess who was at the back of this attack, and it was therefore quite possible that he had outguessed Lance and knew that he was either alone there among the trees or had only the barest handful of men with him.

Throwing himself sideways, Lance slid from the saddle, hit the ground with a bone-crunching blow that knocked almost all of the wind from his lungs, then rolled to the side several times until he had reached the shelter of a clump of tall trees with thick, tangled underbrush around their trunks. There was the savage sound of a second rifle shot from the direction of the rocks, but by the time the echoes had died away among the pines he was worming his way forward, along the edge of the trail, his gun out of leather, eyes and ears straining to pick out Patten's position.

He attained the cover of the final stretch of brush between him and the open trail, slithered like a snake into the undergrowth, feeling the sharp barbs of the thorns cutting into his arms and legs, tearing through his clothing, as he peered out into the sun-hazed distance, seeking a pattern in the shadows.

Behind him, on the trail, he heard the sorrel snicker, and wrapped caution around himself as he lifted his head carefully, an inch at a time. Filling the empty chambers of the Colt methodically, he thumbed back the hammer, waited patiently for the other men to show themselves, determined not to give away his new position by shooting at shadows.

A swift glance told him that more than half of Patten's force had been finished by the twin blasts of the explosive hidden carefully among the rocks. Now it was just possible to see the full extent of the damage caused by the thunderous force of the dynamite. Rocks had been lifted high into the air and lay across the trail, almost blocking it entirely. Other boulders had been split and shattered, the fragments of rock hurled with the force of bullets into the bodies of the men caught by the blast.

Those gunhawks still alive were clearly in no mood to continue the fight. A few desultory shots whistled into the trees around him, humming like a swarm of angry hornets over his head, but although Patten yelled hoarsely at them to turn their mounts and ride him down, the threats uttered by the rancher seemed to be having no effect.

Lance smiled grimly to himself in the shadows of the thicket. Aiming deliberately, he sent more shots cutting into the group of men struggling to get their frightened mounts back across the stream. Out of the corner of his eye he caught a fragmentary glimpse of Patten, moving back among the tumbled boulders. A snap shot missed the other by inches, whining off the hard rocks, sending the rancher sprawling sideways, seeking cover.

Dropping down out of sight, Patten yelled hoarsely: 'I ain't finished with you yet, Turner. I'm going to ride you down no matter where you try to hide in Vengeance. I'll hunt you down and watch you squirm before I hang you from the most convenient limb.'

Lance blasted off another shot in the direction of the other's voice. Just beyond the creek he could see the riders, their mounts under control now, bunching together. He swung the long-barrelled Colt to cover them, then eased his finger reluctantly off the trigger. There was no point in wasting lead trying to kill any of them, he decided. They were beyond the range of the revolver. Had he brought the high-powered Winchester with him it might have been a different story. From that distance he could have brought several of them down, including Patten if he stepped out of the cover of the rocks and tried to make a break for his own mount.

'Better ride back on to your own spread, Patten,' he called sharply, his words carrying easily in the ensuing silence. 'There is no place for you or your kind in Vengeance. If I see you or any of those gunslicks with you in town wearing guns, I'll shoot you down on sight. Don't say I didn't give you fair warning.'

'You're warning me!' Anger and frustrated hatred and fury distorted and blurred the other's words as he spoke up from somewhere among the rocks. 'You may figure that you've been goddamed smart and that you've stopped me with this low-down trick of yours, but you're wrong. Before tonight, Turner, at sundown, I'm coming into Vengeance. When I leave you'll be lying dead in the street or hanging from a rope's end. I promise you that.'

It was no idle threat. Lance knew that instinctively. Crouching down in the brush, he watched as Patten emerged from the rocks overlooking the creek, clambered unsteadily on to the trail and saddled up, one of the men holding the skittish horse steady by the reins. The other paused for a brief moment, staring back along the trail, eyes slitted against the glare of the sunlight glancing off the rocks. Then, savagely, he touched spurs to the horse's flanks and swung away, back along the trail towards the Lazy K ranch, those of his men who were still alive falling in behind him.

Slowly, wearily, Lance pushed himself upright. Sweat and grit had worked their way into the folds and creases of his flesh, rough and irritating. He wiped his mouth with the back of his hand. His lips were dry and cracked, parched already by the blistering heat, and several moments fled before the tension in his body eased sufficiently for him to get to his feet.

Cautiously he went forward, the Colt still poised in the palm of his hand, ready for instant action. But none of the men lying where they had fallen stirred as he touched them with the toe of his boot. Finally he holstered the gun, and made his way back to the waiting sorrel.

Under the trees the air still held a residual coolness. It was a deep green world through which he rode slowly, absorbed in his own thoughts, trying to clear things up in his mind. By now Patten had only half a dozen or so men still riding with him. If only the townsfolk in Vengeance would back him now, victory was undoubtedly theirs for the taking. Even as the thought passed through his mind, he knew that they would never believe him if he tried to tell them that. They would consider it merely bluff on his part.

At the back of his mind, he knew that Patten would not ride far before he turned and headed back towards Vengeance. As soon as he had talked those men with him into riding back to carry out their mission of revenge, they would be hard on his trail. No time in which to get word through to Diego and the other ranchers. It would take far too long to round them all up, even if they were willing to return to Vengeance and help him again.

All of his thoughts were bleak as he came out of the thick timber into the strong yellow sunlight that flooded over the trail, washing most of the colour out of the surrounding territory. His body was weary and his brain seemed to be working only sluggishly so that, for a long while, he allowed the sorrel to pick its own pace and have its head, not thinking, content to sit easily in the saddle and ignore the bruises and aches in his limbs. It seemed impossible to remember when he had last had a good night's sleep.

He deliberately cut west as he left the rough, rocky trail a quarter of a mile further on, came across a narrow, fast-running stream and paused to let the horse drink, getting down and washing the dust of the trail off his face and neck. The touch of the cool water on his flesh made him feel better. Swinging back into the saddle, he rode slowly on, the sun in his face as it reached up to the zenith, a burning disc in the cloudless arch of the heavens, throwing only small shadows now.

The showdown was almost on him and he felt strangely at ease. Now that it had almost come, he knew exactly what he was up against. Patten and perhaps six gunmen, riding into Vengeance in an attempt to cut him down, and not one of the townsfolk had the guts to lift a hand to help him.

None of his movements now had haste and yet every one of them counted. He found his way downward through more pines with the deep green carpet of needles shed over many years forming a thick layer underfoot, muffling the sound of the horse's hooves. Here was where he joined the lower trail that cut into Vengeance from the east, the trail he had ridden with Herb Keene when he had gone out to meet the other ranchers, the lower trail which, at this point, wound through almost the exact centre of a wide valley. Here, he thought, with a sudden realization, he made an excellent target for any dry-gulcher up there in the hills with a high-powered rifle. But he was relying on Patten wanting desperately to shoot him down in the streets of Vengeance in full view of the towns-folk, and not out here in the open; wanting to humiliate him, wreak all of his revenge on him for what he had done in the past.

Ahead of him Vengeance lay sprawled on the hard plateau of ground. He rode in along the narrow alley that cut across town between the rows of old, tumbledown buildings until it intersected with the main street opposite the front of the tall hotel. Deliberately he kept the sorrel in the middle of the alley, eyes alert. It was improbable that Patten had already ridden into town, but there was the chance that one of the townsfolk might have a try at killing him from cover. They were mostly Southerners and he knew and understood their fierce and deep-seated pride. When they had made him marshal, although they had clearly not known it at the time, they had caught a wildcat by the tail and now they were trying to figure out some way of letting it go before it was too late.

He wondered briefly if any of them had heard those rumbling echoes to the north of town. If they had, there was just the chance that they might be asking themselves what could have happened out there and how had the marshal come riding back alive when Patten had sworn to kill him.

The alley was deserted. He rode past the warehouses and the stinking place where the hides were stretched out drying in the sun, then on past Benson's office, pausing to throw a swift glance through the windows, but there was no sign of life inside. Even when he turned into the main street itself, he could see little sign of life. A couple of men lounged in front of the saloon, sitting back in the high-backed chairs, their booted heels resting on top of the rail, but he noticed with a wry smile that they both gave him a quick apprehensive glance, enigmatic and veiled, as he rode slowly by, holding the reins loosely and easily in his hands, then they hurriedly got to their feet and vanished inside the saloon, the doors swinging shut behind them.

He chewed his lower lip thoughtfully. The tension was already beginning to mount. Vengeance lay quiet and still, too still, in the heat of the afternoon, but it was an uneasy silence that seemed to press down in all directions, squeezing itself like a twisting hand among the buildings, something which could have been cut with a knife, it was so thick and tangible.

EIGHT

GUN WOLVES

Reining his horse, he slid wearily from the saddle, tethered the sorrel to the post in front of the sheriff's office and went inside.

Out of the corner of his eye, he saw the clerk standing in the open doorway of the hotel. The moment the other became aware of Lance's gaze on him he whirled swiftly on his heel and went inside. A moment later one of the heavy curtains over the lower window twitched as if a hand had drawn it slowly aside. He formed a grim smile on his lips as he stumped into the office. So he was being watched, was he?

The anger began to bubble up inside him again, something which he could barely control now. A town that wasn't worth saving, and yet he had to save it, even if it meant losing his own life in the attempt.

Pushing back his hat, he went through to the cells at the rear of the building. The three prisoners were lying on their metal bunks, staring up at the flat ceiling over their heads. They eyed him with a sullen amusement as he paused in front of the cells.

'You still around, Marshal?' asked one of them with a coarse laugh. 'We figured you'd have taken your chance and ridden out by now. Reckoned that it was Patten coming along to open up the cells and let us out.'

'Then you were mistaken, weren't you?'

The grim, black-bearded man nearest him shrugged his shoulders negligently.

'We can wait,' he said thickly. 'We don't think we're mistaken, that's all, Marshal.'

'Could be that you'll all be mighty interested in what I've got to say, then.' Lance spoke softly and evenly. 'Most of Patten's men have been killed a few hours ago on the trail leading north.'

The big man stared, then stopped, still grinning.

'You can't fool us, Marshal. You couldn't stop them all by yourself, and we know for sure that those rancher friends of yours have ridden out of town to look after their own spreads. Seems they ain't so sure you can protect 'em against Patten.' His teeth showed in a savage, snarling smile.

'Could be that you didn't hear those two explosions here, then,' Lance said harshly. 'Patten wasn't too clever. He never figured there might be a trap to stop him and his bunch before they got here.'

'Explosions?'

There was an odd edge of tension to the other man's voice now. He no longer seemed to be quite so sure of himself. Clearly this was something that had not occurred to him.

'That's right. Seems one of my rancher friends had some dynamite from the time when they were blasting the railroad tunnel to the east of town. I managed to put it to even better use.'

A pause while the other men digested this piece of news. Then the big man gave a short, derisive snort.

'You expecting us to believe that story, Marshal?' He shook his head slowly and ponderously, came forward and gripped the steel bars with both hands, thrusting his face up against Lance's. 'If that was true, the townsfolk would have been here by now and you know it, storming the jail, trying to get us out for a lynching party. But they haven't come. And they won't. And you know why, Marshal?

Because Patten is still alive and he'll soon come.'

Lance stared at the other for a long moment, his right hand very close to the butt of the gun in the leather holster. Then he forced himself to relax, stepped back and made his way along the passage into the outer office.

Slowly the minutes were ticking away. The sun had passed its zenith now and was beginning to slide down the clear dome of the sky towards the western horizon, throwing longer shadows across the street, although the terrible heat head still persisted. There was the sudden sound of footsteps on the boardwalk just outside the office and a moment later the door opened and Keene walked in, paused for a moment in the doorway staring across at him.

Lance noticed that the other carried a rifle over his shoulder and he had two heavy Colts tied down at the waist. He looked a ludicrous figure standing there, scarcely able to stand upright for the weight of artillery he carried.

'Heard you'd ridden outa town this morning at dawn, Marshal,' greeted the other.

He walked into the office, closing the door behind him after throwing a swift glance along the street in both directions.

'Figured you must have had something on your mind to go riding out like that alone, with Patten ranging the prairie looking for you.'

'I did.' Lance gave a quick nod. 'I got that dynamite and laid it on the trail yesterday, then went out and blew it in their faces this morning when they came riding for town.'

The old man's eyes lit up at the thought. He grinned, took a thick black cigar from his pocket and proceeded to blow clouds of evil-smelling smoke into the room.

'Patten still alive?'

'Afraid so. He let his men cross the creek first. Seems the devil still looks after his own as far as he's concerned.'

'And he'll still be riding into town?'

'Sure. Reckons he'll be here to gun me down at sunset.'

'Well, I reckon the two of us ought to be able to finish him, no matter how many gunslicks he brings with him this time.'

'He'll only have half a dozen at the most. The others are lying out there among the rocks. But you won't be meeting them with me, old-timer.'

'And why not?'

The other stared at him with a look of indignation on his seamed features. 'Do you reckon I don't know how to handle a gun? I ain't scared of these killers if the rest of the folk in town are.'

'I know you're not.' Lance nodded his head quietly. 'But you don't stand a chance against professional killers like these. Besides, this is now something personal between Patten and me. I've got to see it through my way or not at all.'

The other sank down into the chair in front of the desk.

'You're a danged fool, Marshal.' he said throatily. 'Don't know what to make of you. Yesterday you went all over town trying to get somebody to back you up, somebody you could deputize. Then when I come along, you don't want me.'

'Don't get me wrong, Herb.' Lance got to his feet and walked around the side of the desk. 'It isn't that I don't want you, but I'd always have to be keeping an eye on you, and in this showdown that isn't going to be possible.'

'But you can't fight seven men by yourself. They'll take you from the side, and that'll be the finish.'

Lance pursed his lips.

'I'm not so sure about that. They'll be cocksure of themselves, and that will make it easier to stop them.' He stared coldly out of the window. 'Besides, I reckon everybody here is going to keep off the street. That means when they do come, I'll be shooting at everybody who moves out there. I wouldn't like to shoot you down in mistake for one of those polecats.'

'You got no objections if I stick around the office, just to back you up if things get a little rough?' There was a note almost of pleading in the old man's voice.

The long afternoon wore on. The heat haze that lay over the town did not begin to diminish until the sun was reaching down for the tips of the tall hills on the western skyline. But the streets were still quiet. There were men in the saloon. Lance could just hear their talk from the front of the office, and once or twice he had seen some of the storekeepers make their way over to the hotel but, apart from that, the street remained empty.

There were no drovers in town that afternoon, and Lance wondered in a vague sort of way how they managed to get wind that there was going to be trouble flaring up at sundown. It was as if some sixth sense warned them that guns would be flaming in the streets of Vengeance before the night was through.

He settled back against the wall of the office, squatting on the narrow boardwalk, keeping an eye on everything that happened. The wood was hot against his shoulder blades.

At the prospect of the showdown his nerves tingled a little in his body and every little untoward sound caused him to jerk upright, hand dropping instinctively to the gun at his waist.

His body felt tense, his eyes hard, and he was as edgy as a tormented rattler. There was the continual feel of eyes watching him from the buildings on either side of the street.

He knew that there was a meeting of some kind being held in the hotel. That was the only reason why most of the townsfolk who counted for anything had gone there, casting swift suspicious glances in his direction as they had hurried across the street.

What could they be discussing? he wondered. Perhaps even now, at the eleventh hour, they were trying to decide on some way of getting rid of him before Patten rode into town.

Well, let them go ahead with their meeting, let them spill all of their fancy talk, he thought savagely, furiously, it

wasn't going to do any of them the least bit of good. He
had decided on the course of action he was going to take,
and nothing was going to swerve him from it.

Behind him, Keene came out of the office and stood in
the doorway, staring along the street towards the north
end of town. He said quietly: 'Ain't no sign of him yet,
Marshal. Reckon he's going to come?'

'He'll come,' said Lance simply. 'He knows he's got to
come or he's finished as far as his men are concerned, and
once they turn against him, Patten will be as good as dead,
because if they don't get him, he knows that I will.'

It was simply said, but there was the promise of death in
the softly spoken words and, in spite of himself, Keene felt
a shiver go through him as he stared down at the set face
of the man sitting there on the wooden boardwalk, his
shoulders resting against the wooden wall of the building,
outwardly calm and relaxed as if there was nothing about
to happen.

Suddenly there was a movement halfway along the
street. There was a small group of men coming out of the
hotel. Lance recognized Benson, the lawyer, and Doc
Manly. Most of the others were saloon keepers, or men
who owned the stores in town. They hesitated a moment,
then advanced purposefully towards him in a body.

'Looks like more trouble,' observed Keene laconically.
'Wonder what these *hombres* want. I wouldn't trust any of
'em, Marshal. They're a double-dealing lot.'

'Just let me handle 'em,' Lance said tightly.

He got to his feet and stood waiting until the others
paused in the dusty street before the office. Benson
stepped forward.

Clearing his throat noisily, he said:

'I've been elected the spokesman for the town, Marshal.
We've been talking things over, trying to reach a decision
among ourselves as to what would be best for the town.'

'And may I ask what you've finally decided?' Lance
stared at the other coldly, his mouth set into a tight, bitter
line.

'We think that you ought to quit, Marshal. We realize now that you aren't exactly the right kind of man for this job. I'm sorry that we asked you to take it on in the first place, but Sloan had just been killed, and—'

'Why don't you spit it out straight?' said Lance, harshly. 'Sloan was shot down by me because he was a thief.'

Benson coloured deeply and there was a faint filming of sweat on his forehead. He looked nervously round at the men behind him, letting his glance range from one to the other as if looking for support from them. But nobody made a move to speak or back him up and he went on hesitantly:

'Whatever the cause of Sloan's death, Marshal, one thing is quite certain. We do not want this town wrecked and destroyed by Wayne Patten and his killers. We know they'll be riding in soon, looking for you. You don't stand a chance against them and we feel that—'

'God damn you, Benson – and the rest of you. I know myself I should never have taken on the job of town marshal, but not for the reasons you're giving now, but because you aren't worth fighting for, any of you.' His tone lashed them ceaselessly. 'But I don't intend to quit. I don't know how you're so certain Patten is riding into Vengeance, but when he does come, I'll be right here to meet him, and once I've finished this job, I'll willingly turn in this badge. Then, for all I care, the lot of you can rot in the hell of your own making.'

Benson made as if to speak again, then took one look at the hard, rigid face of the man in front of him, changed his mind, and stepped back into the cluster of men in the street.

'That's better,' gritted Lance tightly.

He swept his gaze over the men, knew instantly that there would be no further trouble from them. They might try to argue but that was all.

Then he glanced beyond them to where the sun was already touching the hills, slipping down out of sight. One moment the street there had been empty, deserted. Now there was a small group of men moving in from the far end, grim and purposeful men with a mission. He slitted his eyes against the harsh glare of the red sunlight, then spoke sharply to the men in front of him.

'Looks like this is trouble just coming up.' He pointed with his right hand. 'That could be Patten now. Still want to stay out on the street?'

Benson threw a swift glance over his shoulder, muttered something to the rest of the men, then turned and half-ran across the street into the hotel, the others close on his heels.

From the doorway of the office, Herb Keene chuckled drily.

'Reckon we know who's the cowards around this place, Marshal,' he observed.

'You'd better get in there and stay put,' Lance told him sharply.

He moved forward, keeping into the side of the street where the houses fronted on to it. Moving quickly, he slid down the narrow alley, slipped through one of the buildings there and moved out to the street some fifty yards from the sheriff's office.

He knew, without any conscious thought, that his only chance now was to take these men separately. There was no sense in trying to shoot down the whole bunch at once and with men such as these, killers with a reputation for fast gunplay, there would be no such thing as facing up to him one at a time.

The men had reined their mounts now and were sitting straight in the saddle alongside Patten. From his vantage point Lance could see that the rancher was debating inwardly the best way to take him. He clearly did not want to try anything foolish, knowing how fast and accurate Lance was with a gun. Then he turned in the saddle, spoke to the men with him. As one man they dismounted, slapped their horses across the rump, sending them scattering back along the street.

Then, hitching up their gunbelts, they moved with a

deadly purpose in a single line, spread out from one side of the street to the other, their heels kicking up little spurts of dust as they walked, their hands hanging loosely by their sides, eyes narrowed.

Tension crackled in the breeze that flowed along the street. The whole of Vengeance was a powder keg now, with a smouldering fuse attached – safe enough provided the fuse was long. . . .

Lance edged himself forward a couple of feet, hefting the gun into his hand. This was a time when he did not intend to call any of these men. It was one man against seven and there was only one way now to shorten the odds.

Smoothly he brought up the gun, got his feet under him ready to move fast, his body partially hidden by the wooden veranda. Swiftly he sent two shots into the line of men, knew even as he fired that both bullets would find their mark. Two of the men on either side of Patten stumbled and fell into the dust without a single cry, their guns slipping from nerveless fingers as they tried, instinctively, to swing around and face him.

A fusillade of lead hit the boardwalk, splintering the wooden upright of the veranda as he slithered sideways and was gone like a fleeting shadow, back along the alley and through the building, out at the back, listening for the frenzied pounding of feet that would tell him the others were close on his tail. But although he heard a sharp yell from Patten, there was no sound of pursuit and, as he paused in the narrow yard at the back of the house, thrusting a couple of slugs into the empty chambers of his Colt, he guessed that Patten was not falling for that trick. The other did not intend to rush in and follow him like that, running into another ambush before he knew where Lance was crouched, possibly losing another man.

Carefully he moved forward again, edging away from the main street where he knew the others were, cutting in the direction of the livery stables. Up there, in the upper storey above the stalls, he ought to be able to look down and keep a sharp watch on the street. He skipped across an open space, heard a savage yell from close by, felt the scorching whistle of a slug as it tore along his upper arm, cutting through the flesh but fortunately missing the bone.

He sucked in a deep breath as pain lanced momentarily along his arm. That had been a little too close for comfort.

Behind him he heard the pounding feet now that he had been seen. They knew they had to keep crowding him, that once they lost him again in the maze of small, narrow, twisting alleys that led off the main street, he'd have the chance to strike again without warning. So long as they kept him on the move, on the defensive, they were comparatively safe and sure of themselves.

Ahead of him he saw the livery stables. A bullet chipped a flying fragment of wood from one of the posts of the nearby building as he ran, his body doubled over to present a more difficult target. He heard Patten shout something again, glanced over his shoulder as he ran, saw the two men who burst out from around the corner of one of the buildings less than twenty yards away. One of the men pointed, then staggered as a snapshot took him full in the chest, hurling him back on his heels. He stood swaying for an instant, then fell sideways, bumping against the man who had halted next to him, spoiling the man's aim as he tried to bring his guns to bear on Lance's running figure. Swinging swiftly to one side, Lance saw the bullets from the man's gun throw up little spurts of dust near his feet as he cut diagonally across the street. He was like an animal now, with an animal's instincts. The danger he was in seemed to have sharpened his senses and he no longer was aware of the pain in his arm or the dull ache of fatigue in his body. His breath was rasping in his throat and from the other side of the street now more bullets were wailing in his direction.

He swerved violently, then cut around the corner and was into the livery stable, climbing swiftly towards the hayloft before the first man came into sight around the corner.

Swiftly he threw himself forward, face downward on the straw, and glanced over the lip of the ledge on which he found himself. Down below he heard one of the horses stomping nervously in its stall, knew that it was only a matter of seconds before his pursuers knew why the animal was behaving like that.

'Get him! No matter where he is, get him!' Patten's shrill voice cut across the sudden stillness around the stables.

Glancing down, Lance was able to make out the other's stocky figure near the front of the bank. He had his guns in his hands, was staring about him wildly, trying to make out where Lance had gone. Out of the corner of his eye Lance saw the two men come out into the open on the far side of the street, then sidle across to where Patten stood in the shadows.

Three men dead, four more to go, Lance thought. He could see three of them. Then where was the fourth? There was a nagging worry at the back of his mind as he tried to spot the fourth man, knowing that until he did so he was in deadly danger. For all he knew, that fourth man might be creeping up on him from behind, ready to put a bullet into his back.

He let the air out of his lungs in a soft, barely audible sigh, wriggled forward a couple of inches, then threw caution to the winds, sighted on the men below and loosed off four shots. One of the men dropped in a huddled heap and lay still in the middle of the street. The other three shots went wide as Patten and the remaining gunhawk hurled themselves sideways, out of sight against the fronts of the buildings.

Now they knew where he was and they would come for him. He realized that he had walked into what was virtually a trap. Unless he made his way down that wooden ladder again into the stalls below, he had no other way of escape unless he tried to jump from the ledge some twenty feet above the ground.

He fired at a running shadow at the edge of his vision,

saw the man stumble and then pick himself up again and hobble under cover. A bullet slashed into the woodwork near his hand and he pulled his body back hastily. Let them come, shouted a furious voice at the back of his mind. Let them come into the open where he could see them, let them face him with guns in their hands like men.

But they wouldn't do that. Now they preferred to move in on him from three sides, knowing that they had him trapped, unable to break out of the stables.

He reloaded the Colt, lay waiting for them to make their move. He had cut down their numbers far more than he had ever dared hope. By now the people of Vengeance would be crouching behind doors and windows, not daring to look out for fear of being hit by a stray bullet. But so long as there was shooting, they would know that he was still alive.

From the shadows down below Patten's voice came up to him:

'Throw down your guns, Turner. You don't stand a chance now. We've got you holed up in there and if you don't, we'll come in and smoke you out.'

'Why don't you come in and try to take me?' he called back 'Or could it be that you don't like the odds now that they've been shortened a little.'

A pause, then he heard Patten call: 'Willis. Can you hear me?'

'Sure, boss.'

The hoarse voice came from the other side of the street.

'Get along to the jail and bust out the other three. Then we'll go in and git the Marshal.'

Lance started up. That was something he had overlooked and he cursed himself angrily. He ought to have shot down those three rustlers while he had had the chance. Once they were freed it would take the odds back to where they had been when Patten had ridden into the town. He fired a couple of shots at Willis as he saw the shadowy figure slide out of cover and move off quickly along the street in the direction of the sheriff's office.

'Care to change your mind, Marshal?' yelled Patten.

'Go to hell!' Lance shouted back.

He felt the rage within him rise up again, threatening to consume him completely. He knew there was nothing he could do to stop that man, Willis, from breaking those three killers out of the cells. A bullet in each lock and they would be free.

Then, abruptly, shockingly, there came the blasting roar of a rifle. Not the sharp, clean sound of a Winchester, but the dull, thudding roar of an ancient weapon. Lance's heart gave a sudden leap. Old Herb Keene. He was still back there at the sheriff's office, and he knew he could trust the other to keep a sharp look out. Willis had gone along the street, quite confident that there would be no trouble with the Marshal holed up. He had evidently walked right into the old rancher, and the other would have fired on him without bothering to ask any questions.

'Reckon Willis didn't make it, Patten,' Lance called down. 'I forgot to tell you one of my men was waiting at the office in case of any trouble as far as your three men were concerned.'

A hail of bullets was the only answer from down below. Lance slid back into the piled up straw. There was no time to lose now if he was to get out of this place before Patten pulled himself together and made another move. Sweat dripped continually from his forehead into his eyes and he brushed it away with the back of his hand as he clambered swiftly down the ladder, forcing himself to ignore the pain lancing through his left arm. More fire was being poured into the top storey, but he was safe for the time being.

He moved quickly to the rear stalls, past several which were occupied, out into the wide yards at the rear. Patten and two men still alive, but one of those men wounded. The odds were moving a little more in his favour.

He cut across through vacant lots and tin-can dumps. Behind him the shooting had stopped. Evidently Patten had discovered that he had slipped away and would be moving after him soon.

As he edged forward, the darkness growing about him now that the sun was almost down, he realized that Patten might make straight for the jail. Somehow he had to get those three men out, otherwise there was the distinct possibility of defeat staring him in the face. With only Keene guarding the place, there was a very good chance that he would succeed.

It only needed one of the men to keep the front of the office covered, pumping an occasional shot into the windows, to keep the old-timer on his toes, while the other man, or Patten himself, slipped in the back and released the men.

There was a growing sense of urgency in him as he turned abruptly, cut through a couple of buildings, came out into the street some thirty yards down from the sheriff's office. In the dimness he could see nothing moving, but the whole length of the street had that tense, waiting quality hanging right over it. A little tremor passed along his spine, tightening the muscles of his stomach into a hard, uncomfortable knot. Here, then, he knew, was where it would happen.

Here, if Patten acted as he guessed he would, bullets would come cutting out of the dimness. Here the town would see its marshal die, or live.

Every nerve and muscle tense and taut, his eyes fixed straight ahead, deliberately unfocused so that the slightest movement would register, instantly sending the warning to every part of his body, he stalked forward. A dozen paces and then half a dozen more.

Then there was a sudden movement near the front of the hotel. Lance swung up the Colt to cover it, finger pausing for a fraction of a second on the trigger as he realized that it might be some innocent person moving in that direction.

The flash came even as he flung himself to one side, taking no chances. Then he realized that the bullet had been intended, not for him, but for the front of the office. The gunhawk had worked himself into a position close to the hotel where he could see the front of the office, where it would be easy for him to pump bullets into the windows without exposing himself too much to the inevitable return fire.

The rifle blast echoed along the street. Keene was evidently still alert for trouble, firing over the prone body that lay in the dirt just in front of the building. Willis, thought Lance tightly.

So far, Patten was behaving in an entirely predictable manner. He moved quickly now, reckoning that Keene would have to take care of the man in the shadows. The greater danger would come from another direction entirely, from the rear of the building.

Moving quietly and quickly on the balls of his feet, the Colt in his right hand, finger bar-straight and hard on the trigger, Lance worked his way along the side of the building. At the back he saw that the lock on the rear door, leading directly into the cells, had been smashed by a bullet.

He cast about him momentarily, seeking some sign of Patten in the shadows there, but nothing moved and, throwing caution to the winds, he stepped into the passage, edged along it towards the cells. Narrowing his eyes, he saw the dark shadow standing in front of them, the gun poised in his hand.

Even as he stood there, the man's harsh, rasping voice said: 'Better stand away from the doors. I'll have you out of there in a couple of minutes. Patten is waiting outside. We've lost most of the boys, but I reckon that we'll be able to take care of that pesky Marshal this time. First we'll take that *hombre* in the outer office. He won't be expecting anybody to sneak up on him from behind.'

'That's where you're wrong,' gritted Lance.

He stepped out into the passage, saw the man whirl to face him, the gun lifting in his hand. Then the Colt in Lance's fist spoke loudly and the man tumbled forward into the passage, the gun in his hand blasting a lance of yellow flame as it went off with the final pressure of his finger. The bullet whined off the hard floor and ricocheted into the distance.

'I guess you'll still stand your trial, the three of you,' Lance said tightly.

He backed away, reached the rear door, glanced swiftly into the gloom, then stepped through. Still no sign of Patten. From the street he could hear more gunfire as the man crouched down near the hotel traded shots with Keene.

But where was Patten? Had the other decided that he was fighting a lost cause, with his men either dead or scattered to the wind? Perhaps he had decided to pull out while there was still time, preferring that to a bullet from Lance, knowing that the other would not rest until he had hunted him down.

His mind was cold and calculating as he stepped into the street, looking in both directions. The tight empty feeling in the pit of his stomach increased, and his chest felt cold and clammy. There came one last shot from the direction of the office and then silence.

Probing the dusk, Lance saw the body of the man on the other side of the street, lying sprawled on the steps of the hotel, his arms outflung, his legs twisted oddly beneath him. He knew then that Patten, if he was still in Vengeance, was alone. The odds had finally been evened.

'You all right in there, Herb?' he called sharply.

A momentary pause, then the old man's voice yelled back:

'Sure, I'm OK, Marshal. How many more left?'

'Only Patten, I reckon. I'm going after him. He may try to run for it now that the odds are finally even and he has no men to back him up.'

He made his voice deliberately loud, knowing that the townsfolk would be listening. Slowly he paced along the street, feeling the silence clinging around him, pressing against him from every side. Was Patten hiding in the shadows of the doorways, preferring to shoot him down from ambush, rather than face him man to man? Or had he ridden out of town, back to the Lazy K ranch?

Halfway along the street he caught the sudden flicker of movement among the shadows directly ahead.

'Hold it, Patten!' he yelled harshly.

The other leapt to one side at his shout, spun round and dropped behind the wooden rail along the boardwalk.

Lance moved forward quickly and it was a measure of his concentration that he did not hear the faint whisper of sound as a footstep creaked on the boardwalk at his back until it was too late.

'Just hold it there, Marshal. Don't try to turn around or this gun will go off. I've got a very itchy trigger finger.'

Benson's dry voice! Lance stiffened abruptly. A lot of questions were answered now. He ought to have listened to Keene. The old man had known what he was talking about when he had said that the lawyer was in cahoots with Patten. Now he had fallen into a trap of his own making.

'So you're in this, too, Benson,' he said thinly. 'I ought to have figured you would be.'

'A pity that you didn't, Marshal. I tried to warn you not to go on with this, that you ought to quit and leave Vengeance, but you wouldn't listen. Now you're finished. This is the way it has to be. You know too much. Once we've got rid of that friend of yours in the office back there, and probably Grace Pardee, I reckon Patten and I will be able to continue as we have in the past.'

'So you were the one who shot down Sheriff Pardee.'

'Who else? He was getting a little too nosy for our liking. Besides, like you, there was no way of getting him to obey orders.'

Swiftly Lance tried to think of some way out of this trap, but there seemed to be nothing he could do. In front of him he saw Patten move forward, a trifle uncertainly, then more quickly.

'That you, Benson?' he called.

'Yes. Come on over and keep an eye on the Marshal here. I want to get that man back in the sheriff's office before he causes us any further trouble.'

Patten came forward. He was only thirty yards away now. Glancing down, Lance saw his gun lying in the dirt near his feet. But, as if divining the thought in his mind, Benson said drily:

'Go ahead and pick it up, Marshal. That way we'll finish you like we did Pardee and—'

The rest of his sentence was drowned by the savage roar of a rifle. Lance jerked instinctively, as if expecting to feel the blast of red-hot lead in his back. Then he saw Patten bringing up his guns and, without turning, knowing only that something had happened to Benson, he flung himself down in the dirt, right hand reaching out with the speed of a striking snake for the Colt.

His fingers curled around it even as Patten blasted off his first shot. It ploughed into the dirt within an inch of Lance's hand. Then he had the gun in his palm, brought it up in a swift blur of movement, squeezing off two shots which were so close together that they sounded like one.

Patten stopped in mid-stride, seemed to lift himself up on to his toes as if trying to reach up and lean forward at the same time. There was an expression of frozen aston- ishment and fear on his face as he toppled forward, his body striking the wooden rail, smashing it down with his weight. He toppled into the street and lay still, unmoving.

He let his breath sigh out of him, turning slowly, lower- ing his hand. Benson was sprawled down the steps of the boardwalk, his face upturned to the night sky, where the first few bright stars were beginning to show. But he did not see them. His eyes stared upward, unseeing, his mouth open slightly.

Behind him, on the boardwalk, one arm around the upright, leaning forward, her face as white as chalk, stood Grace Pardee. She stared across the dead lawyer's body at Lance, her lips moving for a long moment before any words came out.

'You heard what he said, Lance. He said he was the man who shot down my father and, from the way he said it, he seemed proud to have done it.'

Lance stepped forward, put his arm around her shoulders. She let the rifle drop from her fingers and it clattered hollowly off the wood on to the dust beside Benson's body.

'You did the only thing you could do,' he said softly. 'He was worse than Patten even, pretending to be your father's friend and then shooting him down in cold blood. You've got no cause to blame yourself for what you did.'

Vaguely, he was aware that the street was filling now. Men came out of the hotel and saloons, staring down at the bodies lying in the street, at Patten a few yards away. Then they came and peered down at Benson.

'Damn this! Damn them all!'

Grace Pardee was murmuring the words ceaselessly under her breath as she clung to Lance, and he could feel the warmness of her through his shirt, her hair was soft under his calloused hand. Then she began to cry, her shoulders heaving as the sobs wracked her body.

Doc Manly came forward. 'Let her cry,' he said quietly. 'It's best that way, she'll get it out of her system quicker.'

'I reckon this town is going to be different from now on,' Lance said, speaking softly to her.

He wasn't sure whether or not she heard him, but after a little while her crying diminished, and she lifted her head, staring up at him, a queer little smile on her face.

'I don't know why I'm acting like this, Lance,' she said softly. 'I always thought I was hard as nails after my father died.'

'Somehow, I don't reckon there'll be any need for you to be as hard as that again,' he said gently. His arm tightened around her shoulders, holding her close.